"Hello, husband,"

Winnie began before hysterical giggles bubbled up from inside her. "That sounds so crazy to me. So unreal. I mean, *older* people are called husbands and wives, aren't they?"

Josh smiled at her affectionately and pulled her close. He brushed his lips lightly back and forth on hers, instantly melting every muscle in Winnie's body. Her knees buckling, Winnie touched her nose to Josh's and slipped her fingers around his neck.

"We're not so young anymore, Win. Are we?" Josh murmured. A gold band that matched Winnie's shone on his finger.

"I guess not," Winnie replied in a tiny whisper.

Shivers were tickling her spine and her face was hot and prickly. Happiness was filling every inch of her body. She wanted to curl up all afternoon with Josh and . . .

Don't miss these books
in the exciting FRESHMAN DORM series

FRESHMAN PROMISES

LINDA A. COONEY

HarperPaperbacks
A Division of HarperCollinsPublishers

This is a work of fiction. The characters, incidents, and
dialogues are products of the author's imagination and are
not to be construed as real. Any resemblance to actual events
or persons, living or dead, is entirely coincidental.

HarperPaperbacks   *A Division of* HarperCollins*Publishers*
10 East 53rd Street, New York, N.Y. 10022

Cover illustration by Tony Greco

First printing: July 1992

Printed in the United States of America

HarperPaperbacks and colophon are trademarks of
HarperCollins*Publishers*

❖ 10 9 8 7 6 5 4 3 2 1

One

"*D a da da-dah. All dressed in white!*"

Winnie Gottlieb pulled open the door of her tiny, off-campus apartment when she heard familiar voices in the hall. A smile spread across her face and her eyes were shining through her spiky brown bangs.

"Hello there, Mrs. Gottlieb," Faith Crowley said cheerfully as she and Winnie's other best friend, KC Angeletti, stepped cautiously into the room. "Or is it Mrs. Gaffey? Ms. Gaffey-Gottlieb? Anyway, we love your funky newlywed look."

"Who cares what they call me," Winnie said

joyfully. "When you're as happy as I am, it really doesn't matter." Winnie lightly touched her polka-dot head scarf and smoothed her flea-market apron with its absurdly large ruffles. "Have a seat."

"You look like something from the *I Love Lucy Show*," Faith said as she set a grocery bag down on the kitchen's dingy Formica counter. Her blond hair was tied back loosely with an embroidered ribbon and her white T-shirt read *Property of U. of S. Drama Department.*

KC looked at Winnie curiously. "So, how is married life? What's it been? Twenty-four hours already?"

"That's right," Winnie breathed, stretching out on a bare mattress flopped on the floor. A giggle bubbled up from her throat and she dusted the air with her turquoise feather mop. "Don't mind me. I'm just going to do a little tidying before my *HUSBAND* gets back from work."

The feather duster stopped in midair when Winnie noticed the worried looks Faith and KC were casting about her apartment. Aside from the half-dozen collapsing boxes overflowing with her clothes and paraphernalia, the apartment was practically empty.

There was the beat-up mattress flopped on

the cracked linoleum floor, a rickety barstool, and a few scraggly plants under the window.

"What do you think, KC?" Faith asked, stepping over an extension cord stretched across the floor.

KC gave the dismal room a cool stare and sat down neatly on the barstool, smoothing her crisp linen slacks. Her long dark hair curled around her striking face and her fluffy sweater was draped casually over her shoulders. "I think," KC said dryly, "that Lauren was in a hurry to get out of here, and I don't blame her."

Winnie gave her a hurt look. "But it doesn't matter, KC. Don't you see?"

Faith's old roommate, Lauren Turnbell-Smythe, had moved out two days before. So when Winnie and Josh suddenly got married, she let them have the place for the rest of the paid-for week. Lauren couldn't wait to return to the dorms after her wealthy parents decided to support her again. She had planned to room with Winnie.

KC sighed. "Poor Lauren didn't count on having Melissa McDormand for a roommate instead of you, Winnie. Melissa must be a basket case now. Can you imagine how Melissa felt yesterday, getting stood up at the altar?"

Faith's face tensed up. "Yeah. It must have been terrible."

Winnie stared at her two best friends. Why were they being so gloomy? Weren't they excited and happy for her? After all, *she* was their best friend. And *she* was the one who ended up getting married to her wonderful, loving soul-mate—computer non-nerdo Josh Gaffey.

Sure, it had been a little unexpected. Most people she knew didn't get married spontaneously when they were only eighteen, and in a wedding chapel that played Elvis tunes, no less. But after she and Josh got lost on a Nevada highway, the wedding chapel miraculously appeared. And instead of asking for directions, Winnie and Josh got married.

Now, everything was different. Winnie could almost feel her old self fading softly away, and her new and better self emerging. Strong. Loving. Patient.

Gone was the crazy, funky, silly Winnie who couldn't take anything seriously. Gone was the Winnie whose grand-scale, outrageous mistakes always made her friends feel sane in comparison.

For once, Winnie knew that she hadn't messed up.

So how long would Faith and KC want to sit around and mourn for poor jilted Melissa?

Winnie heaved another sigh of happiness and lifted her left hand into the air. She stared in wonder at the shining gold band on her fourth finger. Tears began to smart in her eyes just remembering the way Josh's brown eyes had locked onto hers in the wedding chapel's semi-darkness when he slipped it on her finger. It had been so perfect.

"Wake up, Juliet," Faith said, laughing. She grabbed Winnie's hand and lifted her up into a sitting position, where she and KC linked arms with Winnie in a huge three-way hug.

"Just like old times," Faith said. "We're really happy for you, Win. I'm just still catching my breath."

KC took Winnie's hand and looked at the thick, gold wedding band. "It's beautiful, Win. Josh picked out a really nice one. Tell us about it."

"Yeah, spill everything." Faith settled in. "We want every delicious, romantic, sexy detail. What it's like to be an old married lady?"

Winnie suddenly felt shy. Her love for Josh wasn't something she could put easily into words. And talking about it would make it sound like everyone else's love.

And it wasn't. No two people had ever loved each other as much as she and Josh did.

To hide her shyness, Winnie sprang up and began rooting through her boxes. She picked out a plastic starfish and thrust it against her chest dramatically. "First, he carried me over the threshold."

Faith sighed. "No. I thought they just did that in old movies."

Winnie grabbed a bunch of netting, wrapped it over her head, and gave the ceiling a seductive look. "Then we rented a motel room and lit a hundred tiny candles in the bathroom." Her voice dropped to a whisper. "Then we took a long, hot bubble bath."

"Ummm. How romantic," Faith said.

"No kidding," KC agreed, looking wistful.

"Then . . ." Winnie continued with mock-seriousness. "We got into a fight . . ."

Faith's eyebrows shot up. *"What?"*

"With this," Winnie whispered, whipping out a gorilla-shaped water gun. She began playfully squirting KC with it.

"Win . . ." KC laughed, her gray eyes dancing.

"Okay." Winnie smiled mysteriously. "I don't expect you to understand right away. But Josh and I are so happy. He makes me laugh and I make him laugh. It's hard to explain."

Faith got up matter-of-factly and began unloading her grocery bag. "I do understand. But you're going to need to eat. I smuggled you a few choice items from the dorm cafeteria this morning."

"Food? Who needs food," Winnie said, dreamily squirting a dead plant in the corner of the apartment. "We'll live on love."

"Four cartons of milk," Faith continued, ignoring Winnie. "Five packages of Wheaties. Ten pats of butter. Six tea bags."

Winnie stared silently at Faith. Butter? Tea bags? How could Faith be so mundane at a time like this? Didn't she and KC realize that they were witnessing the beginning of a great, lifelong partnership? She would set up a unique network of crisis centers. Josh would design breakthrough computer software. Every morning show would be calling for interviews with America's most remarkable couple.

"Faith's right," KC said. "You've got to start thinking about your everyday needs, like finding a place to live."

"Excuse me while I ignore you both," Winnie replied.

There was a knock on the door, and Faith

opened it. A thin, gray-haired woman stood in the hallway, wearing a faded housedress. She pushed the door open a little and looked suspiciously at KC and Winnie.

"What are you gals doing here?" she asked, peering past Faith. "My tenant's all moved out."

"Hi, Mrs. Calvin!" Winnie leapt up and rushed to the door. "Lauren told my husband and me that we could stay until her lease ran out at the end of the week. Hope that's okay with you!"

"Well, it's not okay with me. But no one asked me. Just be out of here by Saturday," Mrs. Calvin said. She turned abruptly and headed down the stairs. "And leave the place spic-and-span," she shouted.

Winnie shrugged, closed the peeling door, and walked back into the apartment. She noticed that KC had sunk back onto the corner stool and was staring down at her hands. There were smudgy circles under her eyes and her face was drawn.

"Are you okay, KC?" she asked.

"Sorry, Win," KC said, looking shakily down at her long, tapered hands. "I'm happy for you, really I am. But I can't stop worrying about Dad. He's upbeat about his chemotherapy treatments, but . . ." KC broke off, unable to continue.

Winnie rushed over and slid an arm around KC's shoulders. Strong-willed, ambitious KC had always been the one to pull Winnie out of her troubles. But now the tables were turned. Winnie felt a surge of invincibility, as if she had the power to make everything well for her friend, just by willing it.

"Your dad is going to get through this," Winnie insisted, her eyes blazing with conviction. "He's the most positive, loving human being in the whole world. He has what it takes to survive. Doctors will swear to it, KC, even if they can't explain it scientifically."

"I hope you're right," KC said. "It's just that he doesn't seem to be getting any better."

Winnie stared at KC's beautiful, sad face. Her love for Josh had made her feel so strong and sure, there had to be a way she could reach out and pour some of it into KC. She felt so certain about Mr. Angeletti. Wonderful, warm, quirky Mr. Angeletti, with his sandals, his gray hair hanging over his collar, and his sauce-stained chef's apron. When people came into his health food restaurant, The Windchime, they always left feeling that Mr. Angeletti had become one of their best friends. Winnie always figured that was why he had so many steady customers. After all, how many people actually preferred vegetable casseroles and whole wheat spaghetti over, say, a big steak dinner or a pizza.

"Nothing terrible will ever happen to your dad," Winnie insisted. "He's always followed his heart. Look, KC, it's the dull types—like Melissa and Brooks—who attract bad luck. They're the ones who think they have everything under control. And that's why they're doomed!"

"Okay, okay, Win," Faith called out from the kitchen. "I don't know if that's why their wedding fell apart, but—"

"But KC's dad isn't like that," Winnie rushed on, "and that's exactly why he will recover—and why my marriage with Josh is going to be such an incredible success."

"Win?" Faith walked out of the cramped kitchen, holding a huge roll of thick paper. "What's this? Have you taken up painting?"

Winnie smiled and thrust her arms dramatically into the air. *"JOY! EXPLORATION! HAPPINESS!"*

Faith looked at her. "Huh?"

"The Crisis Hotline has a booth at the Health Fair this coming weekend," Winnie explained. She stood up, swept her feather duster to her waist, and took a small bow. "And yours truly is planning to donate a series of unforgettably uplifting banners."

"How are you going to have time?" KC asked tiredly, gazing at Winnie's piles of junk. "Don't you have to find a permanent apartment and move into it this week?"

Faith flopped down next to her and briefly examined the apartment's sagging ceiling. "Yeah, and don't you need time with Josh? And what about studying?"

"You don't understand," Winnie insisted. "I'm overflowing with energy. I can handle everything, including these banners, which are going to be incredible. Everyone will know about the hotline when we're through with that fair."

Winnie looked up when she heard something bump outside the apartment door. Then she saw Josh back slowly in, carefully balancing two overstuffed grocery bags in his arms.

"Whew," Josh panted, tossing his long, dark hair out of his eyes to glance briefly at Winnie, Faith, and KC.

"Josh!" Winnie sprang up and rushed across

the room. He'd only been out for two hours, but already she was longing to be near him again. She longed to watch his smile creep slowly out of the corner of his mouth until it lit up his whole face. She wanted to see his head tilt to the side when he laughed. She wanted to feel the familiar warm wave of love and confidence that swept over her whenever he was near. Winnie had never loved anyone as much as she loved Josh Gaffey.

And the miracle was—that he loved her back.

Winnie snaked her arms around his waist as he set a few overflowing items on the counter. Tucked haphazardly into his jeans was a ragged white T-shirt with a picture of an apple on it that said *Macintosh*.

Slowly, he turned around, lifted her chin up, and gave her a long, loving smile. "Hi, Winnie," he started to whisper before Winnie interrupted him with a long kiss.

Faith and KC instinctively began gathering their things.

"Uh. *Uh-hem*." KC coughed. "We were just leaving. See you two later."

"Bye! Thanks," Winnie said dreamily.

"Don't forget about us, you lovebirds," Faith called out before closing the door quietly.

Winnie waved to them. She was glad to be alone. "Hello, husband," she began before hysterical giggles bubbled up from inside her. "That sounds so crazy to me. So unreal. I mean, *older* people are called husbands and wives, aren't they?"

Josh smiled at her affectionately and pulled her close. He brushed his lips lightly back and forth on hers, instantly melting every muscle in Winnie's body. Her knees buckling, Winnie touched her nose to Josh's and slipped her fingers around his neck.

"We're not so young anymore, Win. Are we?" Josh murmured. A gold band that matched Winnie's shone on his finger.

"I guess not," Winnie replied in a tiny whisper. Shivers were tickling her spine and her face was hot and prickly. Happiness was filling every inch of her body. She wanted to curl up all afternoon with Josh and . . .

"Winnie?" Josh said seriously, unlocking his arms and turning to unpack the groceries. "Mikoto was at our old dorm when I stopped by this morning. He wants three hundred dollars for his old station wagon. What do you say? For groceries? Laundry hauling?"

Winnie sighed. "Actually, I was thinking of

spending the money on a lavish honeymoon hotel suite. We—"

"Are you kidding, Win?" Josh stuck a can of chili on the shelf. "Our cush dorm lives are over. Things are going to be tight enough as they are with groceries and insurance and utility bills and . . ." He whirled around and faced her. "I almost forgot. One of us will have to reverse Lauren's shutoff order at the utility office."

Winnie absentmindedly tangled her fingers in Josh's hair. "I'll do it," she said. "I promise. It's just that—who cares about leases, groceries, cars, and electricity? All that matters now is us."

When Winnie kissed Josh again, she felt his body relax slowly against hers. Her lips were trembling. Her head was reeling. He did understand. He understood everything.

All they needed was each other. Everything else would take care of itself.

Two

....

"Ohhhh. Yuuuuuk," Lauren Turnbell-Smythe murmured, peering under the bed of her new dorm room. It was Monday afternoon, and Lauren was unpacking her things into Winnie's old space in Forest Hall. "Six month's worth of Winnie's old purple bubble gum must be plastered to the bed frame."

Kimberly Dayton, Lauren's friend and Faith's dorm neighbor, shook her head and inspected the inside of Winnie's old closet. "Winnie left in a hurry yesterday, that's for sure. Take a look at this."

Lauren poked her head cautiously into the closet and took inventory. "Look at the junk in here," she said quietly, burrowing her way through piles of stale jelly beans, empty pop cans, and old paperback books. She pulled something out of a dark corner and examined it. "Tiger-striped underwear with a Fred Flintstone earring hooked to the elastic. And finally"—Lauren turned around, holding something carefully away from her with two fingers—"a Hostess Twinkie alive with three different colors of mold."

Kimberly collapsed back onto Melissa's bed, giggling. A pale blue leotard clung to her tall, dark-skinned frame. "Disgusting. Why don't you just put it on the floor and let it walk out on its own? Or better yet, I'll donate it to my botany lab for medical research."

Lauren threw out the Twinkie and stared at Winnie's mess through her wire-rimmed glasses. Remembering that Melissa could return anytime, she nervously moved her boxes closer to her bed. Nothing was more important to her now than a good beginning with her new roommate.

After months alone in Mrs. Calvin's depressing rooming house, she longed for a little companionship. A little conversation. Maybe even the kind of real friendship she had with her last roommate, Faith Crowley.

She couldn't allow herself to fail with Melissa. Nothing could be worse than living alone again, hearing nothing but the dank drip of the kitchen faucet and the lonely sound of traffic in the street below.

"Clean-up time," Lauren announced, rolling up the sleeves of her denim shirt. "Winnie got out of here in a lovesick hurry and left the dirty work to me."

"Yeah," Kimberly sighed. "When you're in love, I guess nothing else matters."

Lauren shrugged and said nothing. After clearing off one of Winnie's forgotten slippers, a bra, and a comic book, she heaved her designer luggage onto the bed and grabbed a broom she'd borrowed from the Resident Adviser. The last thing she wanted to talk about was love. Winnie and Josh could have it. Her disastrous relationship with handsome track-star fraud Dimitri Costigan Broder had broken up a few weeks before, leaving her feeling more lonely and demoralized than ever. To make things worse, her ex-boyfriend, fellow U. of S. *Journal* reporter Dash Ramirez, had been the one who'd uncovered Dimitri's scam of lying about his age in order to stay in university competition.

Now Lauren wanted to forget them both. She was determined to focus on the things she could count on: her writing, her classes, and her friendships.

Especially her friendship with Melissa.

Lauren carefully swept some stray packing material away from Melissa's side of the room. "I have a good feeling about rooming with Melissa, Kimberly."

Kimberly stared at her. "You do? Whew. I don't know. Melissa was always a little tough to begin with. And now she's been dumped by Brooks."

"Things may be a little difficult at first," Lauren admitted, "but I think it just might be my lucky break that Melissa—and not Winnie— will be my roommate."

Kimberly smiled and shrugged. "I hope you're right." She looked absently out the window and sighed. "It's just so sad. Melissa looked so beautiful in her wedding dress."

Lauren set the broom down, took a deep, shaky breath, and unzipped a suitcase. Melissa, more than anyone, would understand her new get-serious attitude. So maybe Brooks *had* walked out on her. Her new roommate was too strong and disciplined to let even a canceled wedding upset her life. Melissa had more important things to focus on, like maintaining her stratospheric grade-point average in the pre-med program. Not to mention her track scholarship, which paid for her tuition.

Lauren began eagerly stacking piles of sweaters and pants onto the bed. She could feel her heart pumping with energy. She would be fine. Her finances were comfortable now that her parents had decided to support her again. She'd been able to quit her drecky chambermaid job and dreary apartment. Her articles for the *Journal* were winning awards. And her writing was better than ever.

She could hardly wait for her new roommate to arrive.

Lauren and Melissa.

They'd be two tough women who had seen it all. They were ready to hack it in the real world.

"Where's Melissa, anyway?" Kimberly asked, lowering a large carton to the floor.

Lauren shrugged as she closed the last drawer and began unpacking her word processor and creative-writing notebooks. "She's probably burying herself in her work. She slipped in late last night and then left early for her eight o'clock chemistry class."

Kimberly examined the carton dreamily. "I'm beginning to remember this incredible CD player from last fall in Coleridge Hall when we were all brand-new, starry-eyed freshmen." She grabbed a penknife and slit the packing tape. "What ever happened to all those cute guys we met the first week?"

Lauren smiled. "I don't think I looked at any of them. I was scared to death."

Kimberly stretched her long arms up to the ceiling and did two quick pirouettes in the direction of the window. "I was scared, too, Lauren." She giggled. "Only I didn't show it."

"Well, I'm not scared anymore, although I probably still look it," Lauren said as she arranged her mark-up pens, computer disks, and reference books on the shelf above her desk.

"Part of the problem," Kimberly continued, as if she hadn't heard a word Lauren had said, "was that I didn't really know what I was looking for in a guy."

"Oh?" Lauren said politely, quietly wondering where she was supposed to hang her towels.

The only rack was on Melissa's side of the room. "What are you looking for now?"

Kimberly crossed her long arms and gave Lauren a mischievous smile. "Well, for one, I'd take Derek's good looks and brains." Her face turned serious, remembering her flaky ex-boyfriend and their recent breakup. "But if I detected an *ounce* of Derek's jealousy or lack of punctuality—forget it."

"So what's the latest on your secret admirer?" Lauren asked, wiping her dusty desk with an old sock. For several days now, someone had been leaving affectionate notes and flowers under Kimberly's door. "Any more floral deliveries or love notes?"

"No," Kimberly replied, "but as soon as I find out who he is, I'm going to subject him to my strict perfect-male test. He must be funny, tall, and athletic." Kimberly settled herself on Lauren's bed and playfully hugged a fuzzy pillow. "I just wish I knew who he was! Is it the cute guy in my botany lab who wears the preppie polo shirts? Or the guy . . ."

Before Kimberly could finish, the door suddenly opened and Melissa walked in. Wearing faded navy sweatpants and an oversized T-shirt, she looked light-years away from the radiant bride in white she'd been the day before. Her wavy, shoulder-length red hair drooped over her slightly swollen eyes, and her skin was pasty white beneath her freckles.

"Hey," Melissa said in a flat voice, dropping a white freezer bag on her desk and flopping onto her bed. She flicked on her reading light and buried her nose in a track magazine.

Lauren sat down self-consciously on her bed, smoothing out a wrinkle on a blanket that lay folded next to her. She looked at Melissa, trying to arrange her face into an expression she hoped would look both cheerful and sympathetic. "Hi, Melissa. Well. Here I am. At last."

"Yeah," Melissa muttered, looking up briefly. "Don't mind me."

Lauren and Kimberly exchanged glances as Melissa turned over on her side, away from them.

"I've got to be going," Kimberly said softly, touching her hand to Melissa's shoulder. "Let's get together, soon, huh? I'm thinking about you."

Lauren shifted uncomfortably on the bed when Melissa didn't answer. She looked desperately at Kimberly who was opening the door. "Uh, listen. Thanks a lot, Kimberly, for helping me move all this stuff."

Kimberely nodded and shut the door behind her. Now Lauren had to deal with the silence on her own. She watched as Melissa began flipping rapidly through a magazine.

Snap. Flip. Crackle. Flip back. Flip forward.

Lauren stood up and quietly resumed her unpacking. Did Melissa want to talk? Or should she be as quiet as possible? Lauren racked her brain, trying to remember the exact feeling she'd had after breaking up with Dash. When she glanced back, she saw Melissa staring glumly into space. Their eyes met briefly.

"Mind if I set up your TV?" Melissa asked. Her green eyes looked vacant and tired.

"No. Please. Set it up anywhere you like," Lauren said quickly.

Melissa got up, dragged the television over to her side, and plugged it in. Settling herself inches away from the screen, she flicked on a mindless game show and pulled out a quart of ice cream from the freezer bag. After covering her knees with a blanket, she opened up the ice cream carton and dug into it with a large spoon.

Lauren continued unpacking her books, feeling more and more like an intruder in her new room.

"AAAHHHHNNNNNNGGGGGGG. Your

*answer is wrong, Cheryl Jacobsen of Fargo, North
Dakota! And now an important message from
Florocare Beauty Products . . ."*

Lauren winced at the blaring game show
buzzers and screaming contestants. Was this the
same Melissa McDormand who practically used
to sprint from class back to her dorm room so
that not a moment of precious study time
would be wasted?

*"The only solution to tired and worn out hair is
our special coconut shampoo,"* a perky voice on
the television announced.

Lauren looked over at Melissa again, just in
time to see her jam an upside-down spoonful of
chocolate chip ice cream into her mouth.
Slowly, she drew out the spoon, making little
sucking noises.

Was this the same person who carefully plot-
ted her study and work-out hours weeks in
advance? Who would meticulously regulate her
protein, fat, and sugar intake, indulging only in
protein-rich power bars when everyone else was
eating peanut butter cookies and sour cream
onion potato chips?

*"And now the moment we've all been waiting
for. Now, for twen-tee-five thooooouuuusand
dollars . . ."*

Melissa slid open a nearby desk drawer and pulled out a squashed candy bar, which she opened noisily and broke into little pieces over the ice cream in the carton.

Suddenly, Lauren could stand it no longer. "How are you doing, Melissa? Anything I can do?"

"Thanks," Melissa said without looking up, "but no."

There was a long silence.

"Mind if I put my CD player here? You can use it anytime, Melissa," Lauren said, earnestly looking her way.

"No. I don't mind."

As quietly as she could, Lauren began unloading her clipping files and writing supplies. But the longer she stayed in the room, the guiltier and more uncomfortable she felt.

"I'm really sorry about what happened," Lauren finally said. "Have—have you talked to Brooks yet?" Lauren could see the expression on Melissa's face harden, and she had a sick feeling she'd said the wrong thing.

"Thanks. And no, I haven't heard from him," Melissa said curtly, glaring at the TV screen. "He's gone back to Jacksonville to be with his family. Meanwhile, I'm stuck here. I feel awful.

This is the worst week of my life. Any other questions?"

Lauren felt a sick lump harden in her stomach. The room felt small, hot, and more foreign than ever.

"No," Lauren whispered, too upset to say anything else. Quietly, she gathered her purse and headed for the door, driven by a sudden, crazy impulse to run back to her grim neighborhood, where she could be alone in her apartment.

But then she remembered.

She was back in the dorms for good, and she'd have to learn to get along with Melissa. It was like a replay of the fall of freshman year when she'd first arrived on campus—weary, hollow, and friendless.

Over on sorority row, Courtney Conner stole a quick glance at herself in the mirror before heading downstairs for the Tri Beta sorority's weekly Monday meeting and dinner.

As usual, her shoulder-length blond hair was pulled back gracefully with a tortoiseshell headband. Her immaculate, powder-blue jacket rested primly over a matching floral skirt.

On her desk lay the fifteen-page report she had just completed for her international economics class. Neatly propped up next to it was her calendar, filled with dozens of dinners, parties, meetings, and classes she had coming up for the rest of the month.

She sighed.

If everything is so under control, why do I have this nagging feeling that something is missing? she asked herself silently.

Courtney slipped a clipboard under her arm, left her room, and headed down the freshly vacuumed hallway. As expected, everything in the venerable Tri Beta house was neat, polished, and squeaky clean. After all, it was the first Monday of the month—clean-up day. The day she'd personally designated last fall as Tri Beta Pride Day. And her sisters had followed her orders scrupulously.

So why do I long to see something out of place?

She stopped at the top of the Tri Beta's grand staircase and stared down at a gathering of sorority sisters admiring an arrangement of tulips and daffodils in the front hall. As expected, everyone was dressed in spring shirtwaists and pretty pastel suits. It had been Courtney, at the beginning of the year, who'd reminded everyone to dress for these weekly dinners.

So why do I suddenly want someone to show up in an old pair of sweatpants?

"Hi, Courtney!" called out eager-beaver Marcia Tabbert, who was unfailingly attentive to Courtney, whether she was gushing over her new sweater or repeating one of Courtney's clever remarks. "We're ready when you are!"

An unfamiliar wave of doubt swept through Courtney. Her Tri Beta sisters stuck to the rules, all right. But the most important rule *wasn't* in the Tri Beta's lengthy Code of Conduct: Stay on good terms with the president—at all costs.

Now she was beginning to wonder what her sisters were *really* like when she wasn't there.

In the last few weeks, in fact, Courtney had begun to feel as if she were on stage—in front of a huge audience, walking through a carefully scripted play she had written, directed, and was starring in herself. Her Tri Beta sisters were merely wearing the costumes she had selected; rehearsing the lines she'd written; even walking through a special set she'd designed.

Courtney stared absently down the staircase and dug her heels into the plush oriental rug.

She was suddenly filled with an eerie sensation that none of it was real.

"Courtney?" Marcia looked up with a polite, questioning smile. "Are you all right?"

Courtney blinked, slipped quickly down the stairs, and gave the group a quick, hurried wave. "Just a few more minutes and I'll join you."

Suddenly, nothing was making any sense.

That's when Courtney spotted her friend KC, alone in the dining room, trying to fold a stack of linen napkins into flower shapes. At least KC was in touch with reality. She'd been accepted into the Tri Betas on the strength of her brains and personal style. And she'd always had real-life difficulties to overcome: financial problems, a recent flirtation with drugs, and now her father's terrible illness.

"You look confused," Courtney said, relieved she'd found her. "Did someone put you on fancy napkin duty?"

KC looked up and nodded. She looked pale and serious, but her long dark hair still curled perfectly about her beautiful face. "Diane wants them to look like calla lilies."

Courtney dumped her clipboard down next to her and began folding, too. "I'm really glad you're back, KC," she said. "For a while there, I thought we'd lost you."

KC pressed her lips together. "I thought I had it together, Courtney. But it all fell apart. And the pills and drugs just made things worse. Now I don't even know who I am anymore."

Courtney flared the edge of a napkin out expertly, then set it down, looking closely at KC's pale profile. "I have a feeling you need us, KC. Now more than ever."

"Put me to work," KC said, anxiously running her fingertips around the edge of the glossy mahogany table. "Organizing. Fund-raising. Anything."

"There's always plenty to do, KC," Courtney comforted her, feeling her friend's anguish, but also stirred by the real-life drama that was going on in KC's life. At least KC was dealing with something important. A serious disease. A possible death in the family. It was a far cry from her other sorority sisters' worries over clothes, dates, and fitting in.

KC knew what was important. Maybe that was why Courtney trusted her. KC had never fawned all over her just to be accepted. She knew she didn't have to.

"Meeting's in one minute," Courtney sighed, slipping an arm around KC's elbow. She tilted her head in KC's direction. "Let's hope this one moves along really fast. I'm not in the mood."

When the two arrived in the elegant living room, the Tri Beta sisters were quietly gathered around a pretty spring vegetable platter, chatting politely and sipping chilled glasses of iced tea. Courtney strode into the room and confidently took her place in her usual cream-colored wing chair.

When everyone sat down, a sea of pleasant, attentive faces turned Courtney's way, eagerly awaiting her first words.

"Thanks for coming, everyone," Courtney began, staring blankly at a large oil portrait hanging above the mantel, feeling more bored every second. "The main item on our agenda tonight is our annual spring fund-raiser. It's coming up in only three weeks, so we've got a lot of work to do in very little time."

Courtney watched the Tri Beta sisters' faces take on uniform expressions of concern and dedication.

"Let's come up with a really original idea this year," Courtney continued, trying to sound enthusiastic.

The Tri Beta sisters looked instantly enthusiastic.

"Anyone have any fun, witty, creative fund-raising ideas?" Courtney asked.

Everyone tried to look as if they were deep in thought.

"I've got an idea," Tri Beta secretary, Diane Woo, spoke up. "Alumni weekend is coming up in exactly three weeks and it's going to be big. It's the twenty-fifth reunion for one of the tightest and wealthiest groups in Tri Beta history."

"You're not kidding," sophomore Elizabeth Blythe spoke up. "My mother's one of them. It's her biggest event in five years. Bigger than the arboretum's flower show! Bigger than the museum's costume ball!"

"Why not go all out for these ladies?" Diane continued, laughing good-naturedly with the rest of the group. "Throw an enormous dinner-dance, and auction off some of those old dance cards and photographs sitting up in the attic. We could even piece a quilt and see how high the bidding goes. We'd raise thousands of dollars and generate a lot of goodwill."

Courtney watched her sisters nod their heads in enthusiastic approval.

"Great idea," said Stephanie Bridgemont, a new pledge from a wealthy real estate family in Denver. "My mom will be there and she wouldn't hesitate to show off with an outrageous bid."

"I love it!" another spoke up.

Courtney remained silent and watched the group quietly show their support. It was, without doubt, the best fund-raising idea she'd ever heard of. It was fun and fresh and had the potential to raise thousands of dollars. All they needed was her nod of approval.

But a wild thought suddenly blazed crazily through her mind. It was terrible and wrong, she knew. But it was irresistible.

Courtney gripped her clipboard tightly. What if *she* happened to suggest an idea? Would they stick with Diane's? Or would they side with her, to please her, at the expense of the sorority?

Unable to stop herself, Courtney quickly racked her brain for the most boring, mundane fund-raising idea she could think of.

"I have another exciting idea," she said over the murmur in the room. "How about a rummage sale?"

The room fell silent. Courtney tried to maintain a straight face while, across the room, Diane was trying to control her shocked, hurt expression.

"But, Courtney," Diane ventured cautiously. "I thought you were looking for something orig—"

"It'll be fun," Courtney interrupted. "We've never held a rummage sale before."

Courtney waited patiently for someone to laugh or contradict her. She watched the Tri Beta sisters' eyes shift between her and Diane. The tension in the room was so thick it was crackling.

"Well . . ." Stephanie began, "it's kind of a nice old-fashioned idea . . ."

"Nothing wrong with a rummage sale . . ." Lisa Jean McDermett, another pledge, said softly.

"Tried and true . . ." said Marcia Tabbert, trying to sound convincing.

KC sat up straight in her chair. "A rummage sale, Courtney? I thought you wanted originality!"

"I think it is original," Courtney said boldly, trying to avoid KC's puzzled look. "That's the point. It's so old—it's new! Now, let's vote. How many for the rummage sale? May I have a show of hands?"

Courtney's stomach felt sick as she watched the reluctant hands go up. Only KC and a few senior Tri Betas sided with Diane. The rest passively followed Courtney's ridiculous idea.

"Well then, a rummage sale it is!" Courtney said with a bitter edge in her voice. "Maybe we can take a look at Diane's idea next year."

As the Tri Betas rose to their feet and headed quietly for the dining room, Courtney sat dazed in her seat, unable to move. Were they really that spineless? She could hardly believe it. And that wasn't the worst part. Now, because of her own selfish impulse to control the group and prove a point, Diane's brilliant plan had been squashed.

She wanted to take off her pumps and throw them through the window.

Was there anything left in her life that she couldn't control?

Three

Win, your foot is dangerously close to that can of Coke," Josh said, sitting awkwardly in front of his computer, which was set up on the floor of their temporary apartment.

It was late Thursday afternoon and he was pushing hard to finish a homework assignment for his Computer Science 301 class. He looked over patiently at Winnie, who was sprawled out, painting in the "X" in her "Exploration" Health Fair banner.

"A little dab *here*," Winnie was murmuring to herself. "A dab *there*."

"Winnie?" Josh repeated, returning to his keyboard. "The Coke. Be careful."

The project he was trying to finish was his best ever—a program for a computer game that played like Dungeons and Dragons. Only it had a unique twist that he hoped his professor would go crazy for.

"Huh?" Winnie finally replied, twisting her body in Josh's direction, knocking over the can of soda with her purple sneaker. A long trail of brown liquid headed for Josh. "You want a Coke?"

"Grab a towel!" Josh cried out. Spotting his last clean shirt, he grabbed it and lunged for the puddle seconds before it reached his computer.

"AHHHHH!" Winnie yelled. "Josh. I'm so sorry. Did it get your computer?"

"Close call," Josh mumbled, quietly carrying his dripping shirt to the kitchen sink. He turned around and looked at the apartment in frustration. The small room, which had been practically bare four days ago, was now an ocean of junk.

Overflowing out of plastic garbage bags and boxes were clothes, towels, software manuals, study lamps, camping equipment, and clumps of dirty laundry. Winnie's useless memorabilia, costumes, and junk had been strewn gradually all over the bare wooden floor. Their temporary home had no tables, chairs, or drawers. So between the huge mess and Winnie's art project, the only place left for Josh's computer was a corner of the floor next to the kitchen.

"Let's take a break and clean this place up," Josh said, turning to open the refrigerator. Inside, a leftover slice of pizza lay on a greasy cardboard. There was an opened package of cheese, a half-empty quart of milk, a bottle of Winnie's cologne, and a tub of margarine with the top missing. A rotten banana was squished up against the back.

"Let's clean up when we're done," Winnie answered, preoccupied with painting a bright yellow arrow over her row of letters. "I've got to get this finished and over to the auditorium by tomorrow night. *At the latest*, Saturday morning."

"But, Win . . ."

"Do you like these colors, Josh?" Winnie stood up and stared at her work, apparently not hearing him. "I'm using different shades of blue and green for my Exploration banner because it makes you think of explorers. You know. Crossing the *blue* ocean. Hacking their way through the *green* jungle. But I didn't know these banners were going to be so huge. How will I ever get them on campus?"

Josh stared at Winnie as she cheerfully shoved a pile of dirty clothes closer to the wall, then pounced back to her oversized banner. She didn't seem to mind the mass of confusion in the apartment. But that was Winnie, Josh thought tenderly. Once she decided to focus on something, she poured her heart and soul into it—and forgot everything else.

Click. Click. Click.

Josh bent back down to his work.

1235000000000000000000000000000000000000 0000000.

Josh frowned at the long line of zeroes marching across the screen. Deleting them quickly, he squinted back at the screen.

BEEEEEEEEEEEP, his computer spoke up.

Josh ran his hand through his hair, popped a piece of stale popcorn into his mouth, and punched in a few numbers. The gold of his wedding band caught his eye, and a smile began to slide across his face.

We did it. We really did it, he thought.

He looked over at Winnie, who giggled softly to herself as she painted a face inside a fat, green star.

What was it about her that made him feel so alive and happy? Was it the warm, funny way she drew him out and made him feel like he finally belonged to the world? The way she made even the most mundane things seem curious and exciting? Or was it the bold way she followed her heart—even if it meant risking everything?

Whatever it was, Josh knew his life would never be predictable or boring again. If anything, his life would have more adventure in it, not less.

"Hmmmm." Winnie was humming contentedly as she dotted the top of the banner with a series of aqua polka dots. "Da dummmm."

Josh continued to stare at her. He loved the way her tight Lycra pants fit over her toned body. And the way her oversized, hot-pink T-shirt had been tied at the waist into a funny shape. He felt a rush of tenderness and had an urge to lie down next to her and play with the little spikes in her crazy hair.

"I love you, Win," he said softly.

"I love you, too, Josh," Winnie said, lifting her chin and smiling at him steadily as she dipped her brush into a can of blue paint.

NEEEEEEEUUUUUUHHH. The computer made a strange sound. Josh hunched back over his program, trying to figure out what was wrong.

"Win," he said finally. "Let's clear this stuff up. I've got to find my power surge protector. This wacko electrical system is making me nervous."

"Okay. Give me a minute." Winnie grabbed a stack of Josh's books to weight the end of the banner. "Isn't it weird how everything happens at once? Did I tell you that I've got a French quiz tomorrow? Then Faith and I are going over to the U. of S. Hospital to visit Mr. Angeletti. I can't wait to see him."

Josh stood up, stretched, and peered into the cupboards, hoping they still had the canned chili he'd bought at the grocery store.

"KC's dad is the kind of person everyone wants to get close to," Winnie continued. "It's hard to describe, Josh. But people walk out of his restaurant feeling like they've made a connection. Talking to Mr. Angeletti isn't like talking to just anyone. He's actually listening to you. He actually cares about what you're saying. And so it makes you want to give something back."

"Win? Do we . . ."

"There is *no way* we're going to lose him!" Winnie concluded, not hearing Josh. "He's too vital. He's the kind of guy who lives to be ninety-nine years old."

Josh looked up at the ceiling and shook his head. He was concerned about Mr. Angeletti, too, but his stomach was grumbling with hunger and he still had a long way to go on his assignment.

Flopping down in front of his computer again, he briefly considered going out for a hamburger. He needed to eat something and have a few minutes of peace and quiet, but he knew Winnie would be hurt if he went alone. Plus, if she came, dinner would probably cost them about ten dollars, which they couldn't afford.

Josh sighed and tried to organize his thoughts. Living with Winnie in a small apartment was very different from having her down the hall in the dorm. He couldn't wait until they settled into a larger place where he'd have a quiet room to study in. And a decent electrical system for his computer.

"Winnie?" Josh stretched his long legs out in a V around his computer and began calmly punching his keyboard. "You said you'd stop by the grocery store, but I don't see anything."

Winnie sat up and clapped her hand to her forehead. "*That's* what I forgot. I knew I'd forgotten something. I got extra yellow paint and three marking pens, but I forgot dinner. Wait a minute." She leapt up and began rummaging through her purse. *"Voilà."*

"What?"

"Tuna," Winnie exclaimed. "Two cans of tuna. Faith gave them to me in Western Civ. today. I'm going to make creamed tuna on toast, just like Mom used to make." She went to the freezer and stuck her head in. "Look," she said, holding up a plastic bag. "Hamburger buns. I'll pop them in the old toaster Lauren left for us."

"Winnie, why don't you let me make a couple of sandwiches?" Josh protested.

Winnie tugged something frozen solid in the back of the ancient freezer. "There's ice cream in here, too. We can make milk shakes in Lauren's old blender. I can't wait. This is authentic comfort food, Josh."

Winnie grabbed her old-fashioned ruffled apron and began bustling noisily in the kitchen. Josh checked his watch and bent his head back down to his computer. Winnie continued to talk, boogying to the rhythm of her can opener, and dancing with the open refrigerator door.

After a few minutes, Josh got used to the background noise and focused on his work.

Click. Click. Click.

Maybe it *was* possible to tune Winnie out

when it was absolutely necessary, like tonight.

"And now to thicken up our nice hot creamed tuna," Winnie continued cheerfully.

NEEEEEEEEEE.

Josh leaned back and frowned. There was that weird noise again.

"I'll add a bit of flour, milk, and margarine . . ."

NAAAAAAAAAAAAAH.

Josh glanced up absently, trying to decide whether he should close up his document or take a peek inside his system file. Winnie was busily trying to jam two slices of frozen bun in the toaster.

TAP. TAP. TAP. TAP. TAP. TAP.

Josh decided to keep working until dinner, then check things out. He stared absentmindedly at Winnie dumping icy chunks of old ice cream into the electric blender.

TAP. TAP. TAP.

No problems now, anyway, Josh thought, noticing out of the corner of his eye that Winnie was spreading some kind of tablecloth over a packing box and was setting it with candles.

"Almost ready, Josh," she sang out. "Look at me. I'm June Cleaver. You know, *Leave it to Beaver*?"

"Uh-huh," Josh mumbled, not hearing her.

After three thousand lines of programming code, he was worn out.

"Toast into the toaster," Winnie said, pressing the lever down with a flourish. "And for my final number"—she poised her finger dramatically over the blender's on button—"milk shakes!"

NNNNNNNNNNNNNNNNnnnnnnnnnnn nnnnnnnnnnnnnnn.

Josh looked at his flickering screen in horror. A distinct acrid smell filled his nostrils. *"WIN-NIE!! SHUT OFF THE APPLIANCES!"* he yelled.

"What?" Winnie gave Josh a scared look. "Okay."

Josh continued to stare at his screen as if his life depended on it. He broke out into a cold sweat. "Okay. Okay," he whispered. "It's just a little electrical surge. No reason to panic."

"Lose anything?" Winnie asked nervously.

Josh punched in a disk-save command. "Uh. Well, I should be able to get this thing onto the hard drive and save it," he answered. Silently, he prayed nothing else would happen before his program was locked safely into the hard drive. Just a minute or so would do it.

"Want your creamed tuna while you're working?" Winnie's voice drew closer. "Gee, that toaster really burned the heck out of this bread."

CLICK.

"OH, NO!" Josh screamed. "The power went out."

"I'll light some candles," Winnie said. She groped in the dark for matches and lit one of the candles on her makeshift table.

"Candles aren't going to help, Win," Josh yelled. "My program is gone! Hours and hours of work—gone!"

"I wonder what hap—" Winnie stopped midsentence. "Oops! We didn't contact the utility company about keeping the power on."

Josh stared at Winnie. "But you *promised* you would do it."

Winnie's eyes froze in their sockets. "I forgot," she said, stunned. "I'm sorry, Josh. I guess I'm not very good at remembering the boring stuff."

Josh's face was beginning to get hot. He didn't want to explode at Winnie, but his whole body was starting to shake. "The *boring stuff* is what you have to do to survive, Win."

"I know, but . . ."

"*I'm* the one who's done the boring grocery shopping. *I'm* the one who's buying the boring car," Josh heard himself say. "And *I'm* the one who's cooked every night this week when I could have been finishing this program!"

"You don't have to yell!" Winnie burst out. "You act like I purposely wiped out your program!"

"I don't enjoy drudgery any more than you do, Winnie," Josh said, his anger fanning into a small brush fire. Didn't she understand that they were partners now? Did she think getting married meant that the *guy* suddenly took care of everything? There was no way he could do everything, even if he wanted to. And he didn't.

"There are some things we *have* to do, Win," he went on. "Hell, I can spend twenty-four hours straight programming my robot. And if I didn't care so much about you and school, I'd happily blow all of my cash on a motorcycle and ride it across the country."

"Go ahead and take off then!" Winnie cried out. "Take Alphie with you. Make your stupid robot take care of the details."

Josh stared helplessly at the floor.

A wave of fear shot through his body. *Doesn't Winnie understand what a major decision we've made?* he thought suddenly.

"Look, I'll help more," Winnie spoke up first. "Things have just been crazy lately. Plus, Lauren and I are going apartment hunting tomorrow. So we'll be out of this terrible place soon."

There was a long silence. Josh felt his muscles gradually relax. At least he had a good memory. He knew he'd never forget that program. He'd just have to work over the weekend to duplicate it —wherever they ended up living. He glanced over at Winnie, who was now drooped over her sneakers, fiddling with her silver shoelaces. Her eyes lifted and they gazed at each other tentatively.

Josh sighed and shook his head. He ran his fingers dejectedly up and down the dead keyboard.

"You're really going to find an apartment?" Josh asked. "Promise?"

"I promise," Winnie said firmly. "I won't forget. Tomorrow."

Josh nodded.

"You and Alphie," Winnie said in a tiny voice. "I can just see the two of you together, his little metal hands wrapped around your waist as you barrel down the highway. How romantic."

A smile began to creep across Josh's face. Slowly, Winnie took the burning candle and began to light several others she had set up earlier in the week for a romantic atmosphere.

"Alone with Alphie," Winnie said softly, sliding over to Josh's side. "Let's see. What would you two find to talk about?" She screwed up her face and imitated the robot's whirring, nasal sound. *"NNNNnnnnnuuuuhhhhhh."*

For a few seconds, Josh didn't say anything. Then her shoulder lightly brushed his, and he felt Winnie's warmth—her craziness—getting to him again. Melting him down. Softening him up. Just like it always did.

"EEEEuuuhhhhhhmmmmmmmnnneeeewwwweee eee," Josh whined softly.

"Nnnnuh. Nnnnuh." Winnie began to nuzzle the side of his neck. He could smell her flowery scent. Feel the smooth side of her upper arm sliding against his back.

"Neeeeee. Neeeee," Josh replied.

"NNNNNNAAAAWWWW." Winnie walked her fingers lightly around Josh's neck. She slowly lowered herself down into his lap. In the low candlelight, she was more beautiful than ever. Soft. Glowing. Warm.

"MMMMMMMMMmmmmmmmmmm," Josh murmured back, his throat swelling. He couldn't speak. Instead, he stole his arm around her small waist, found her lips, and slowly forgot everything else.

Four

....

Kimberly felt as if she were dancing in slow motion that afternoon as she happily floated up the steps of the life sciences building. Her botany lab didn't begin for another ten minutes, but she wanted to arrive early.

After racking her brain, Kimberly had finally narrowed her list of mystery-admirer suspects to two hunky guys. Both of them were in her lab and she couldn't wait to get there. She had a funny feeling that today was the day he'd finally reveal himself.

Hugging her Botany 201 lab notebook to her

chest, she smiled and gracefully dodged an intense group of professors and research types lumped near the door of the 1960s-style brick building. A few weeks ago, she would have been totally intimidated by their serious looks and heavy cases. But now she was a successful dancer-turned-scientist.

"Hi, Dr. Maxfield!" Kimberly called out when she saw her botany lab professor look up from the group and give her a friendly nod.

On the outside, she still wore her body-hugging leotards and free-flowing skirts, but on the inside, her life was completely different. Now, when her skills were put to the test, it was in a quiet classroom or a lab smelling of chalk and formaldehyde—not onstage with hundreds of people staring at her. Her grades were high. And her confidence was rising every day.

The only thing missing in her life now was romance. And that problem, she was sure, would soon be solved. Any moment now, in fact, could be the moment of truth.

Kimberly slowed down, gulped, and absently ran her hand through her curly, dark hair. The mysterious notes had been so romantic. So personal and clever. She looked up momentarily, trying to think of what she would say when her admirer finally revealed himself. Lost in these thoughts, she was nearly run down by a stampede of organic chemistry students flooding out of a classroom door.

"This is ridiculous," Kimberly whispered to herself, regaining her balance, but sensing a sudden, oncoming panic. What was the problem? She was feeling the same opening-night dance recital jitters she thought she'd said good-bye to forever.

Spotting a flight of stairs, Kimberly impulsively broke into a light jog and took the steps two at a time. Maybe a quick run would help shake off the anxiety.

"Hey, Kimberly," a low voice called down the hallway just as she reached the top of the stairs. Sam Howard, a tall, blond sophomore, strode down the hall in the other direction. He wore faded blue jeans and a checked shirt. Sam wasn't usually her type, but Kimberly liked the sultry way he tilted his head to the side and closed his eyes halfway when he laughed.

Kimberly's stomach quaked and she gripped her bookpack harder to hide the slight tremble in her hands. Sam was a prime candidate. During last week's work on a particularly complicated cell structure, they had shared a microscope. He had stood so close to her she could almost feel his breath tickle her neck.

"Ready for that pop quiz?" Sam asked, lightly punching Kimberly's shoulder. A shiver ran up her spine. Sam was funny, a little offbeat, and one of the best students in the class. Was it him? Or was he that friendly with everyone?

"I'm ready for anything," Kimberly shot back, smiling and slipping past him through the door-way.

As she headed toward her lab table, a strong arm reached out and stopped her gently in her tracks.

"Wait up!" said a muscular guy wearing a white polo shirt and a pair of khaki pants. "Have you got any good notes from last Thursday's class? I blew it off and now I'm desperate."

"Sure, James." Kimberly flashed him a smile. "I'll get them to you. Then you owe me." She smiled inwardly. Just last week, James Ryder had caught up with her as she walked to the student union, and they had spent a few lively moments talking about reggae music. With his lilting Jamaican accent, long black eyelashes, and tof-fee-colored skin, Kimberly concluded that he was easily one of the best-looking guys on campus. Plus, he was a perfect gentleman. Had *he* sent the beautiful flowers? The lovely note on her door?

Kimberly was agonizing over her mystery admirer as she swung her bookbag onto her lab counter. Piled next to her microscope was a neat stack of shiny slides and a beaker filled with a dull green liquid.

"Nice work, Kimberly," Dr. Maxfield boomed as he walked through the lab's side door, carrying a stack of graded papers, his wrinkled white lab coat flying behind him. He slapped her test paper down. Kimberly closed her eyes for a brief moment, then opened them. It was marked with a big, black A minus.

"All *right*," she heard a friendly voice behind her. Kimberly looked back and smiled. Perched on the counter in back of her was Clifford Bronton, the pudgy double biology-chem major who'd been her lab neighbor since the beginning of the semester. He had a round, dark face and short body that was almost always clad in chinos and oxford button-downs. His wiry, black hair was closely cropped.

"Hi, Clifford," Kimberly said offhandedly, turning away to scan the room carefully for Sam and James.

"You're going to ace this class if you're not careful," Clifford said with a half laugh. "Then you'll have to take organic chemistry. A real five-credit delight."

Kimberly looked over her shoulder and gave Clifford a mild smile. His short legs looked funny dangling from the edge of the lab counter. "I'm up for it."

She was trying to concentrate on finding an excuse to walk casually up to the front of the lab—past either Sam's lab counter or James's. But she didn't want to be rude to Clifford. He was brainy. He was probably her best friend in the lab. And he'd already taken a class from Dr. Maxfield, so he always told her what to expect.

Besides, she liked the way Clifford's eyes laughed behind his steel-rimmed glasses.

"The pinhead got a C," Clifford leaned forward and whispered. Kimberly and Clifford usually started lab by gossiping about Dr. Maxfield or some of the more obnoxious students in the class.

"No!" Kimberly twisted around and giggled. The "pinhead" was their nickname for Alvin Skinner, a thin guy with a bow tie who took every opportunity to tell them about his plans for medical school—in his family's great tradition. "How do you know?"

Clifford shrugged and gave her a wide smile. "It was on the top of Maxfield's stack." He pressed his lips together, suppressing a smile. "Let's go easy on him. He's so uptight and pretentious, you know he's headed for a breakdown."

"And you love it, *Doctor* Bronton," Kimberly said teasingly. "You who've aced every pop quiz, paper, and exam we've had so far this semester."

"Well, thanks very much for noticing," Clifford replied as she turned her head away, just in time to see that James was walking toward the front of the room, where Dr. Maxfield was talking with a group of early arriving students. Kimberly grabbed a pencil out of her purse and headed for a sharpener near the front entrance.

James, however, quickly became involved in a conversation with Dr. Maxfield. And Sam was buried under a textbook, apparently cramming for the upcoming quiz.

"May I have everyone's attention, please?" Dr. Maxfield said, raising his hand. The class quieted. "We're starting today with a look at an unusual cell structure. Would everyone please gather around the front counter?"

Kimberly finished sharpening her pencil. She tried not to think of her secret admirer anymore. After all, neither Sam nor James had acted any differently toward her than they had at the beginning of the semester. Wouldn't she have detected a longing glance cast her way? A sexily raised eyebrow? The barest suggestion of interest? When the class was over Kimberly was still as much in the dark as ever.

After dropping her used lab beaker off at the front table, she walked slowly back to her desk. The thrill of playing detective was gone.

Then she noticed a plain white envelope lying next to her lab notebook. Her heart began to thud inside her chest. It had her name on it. She looked quickly around the room, but everyone was gone. Finally, she tore open the envelope and read the short note inside:

Dear Kimberly,
   Will you forgive me for remaining your secret *admirer for so long? I can't go on like this—and you shouldn't have to either. Meet me at the Health Fair at ten Saturday. I'll be in the Environmental Science exhibition area. You'll recognize me, because I'll be*

*wearing a cowboy hat and a yellow rose in
my lapel, to remind me of you.*

> *Until then, I remain,*
> *Your Secret Admirer*

Kimberly looked up from the note and
grinned. Her secret admirer somehow knew
that she was from San Antonio, Texas. How else
could he have known that she loved cowboy
hats? Or that her very favorite flower was the
state's yellow rose?

"Hi, Courtney! Cute outfit!"
"See you this weekend at the luau,
Courtney!"
"Way to go with Dr. Lamott, Courtney!"
Stepping quickly out of her international economics class and into the warm spring air,
Courtney dodged down a side path that led her
away from the flood of foot traffic headed for
the student union. A soft, warm breeze fluttered
through her loose hair and she was surrounded
by the intoxicating, fresh smell of the just-
mowed campus lawn.
When she rounded the corner of the humani-

ties building, she could see the purple-gray outline of the distant mountains. She sighed and
remembered the carefree day she had spent
swimming and sunbathing in the mountains last
fall with Phoenix Cates, the laid-back, long-
haired freshman she'd dated briefly. It made her
want to jump impulsively in her car and dash up
to that same spot, but, as usual, she had a long
list of duties to finish that day.

"Hi, Courtney!" a blond Phi Delta called out
from his car as she stood at a crosswalk. "All
ready for the big blowout? We've got the little
piggy in the fridge."

Courtney forced a smile and waved as the
guy screeched off down the street. The Phi
Delta's annual spring Hawaiian luau was
Saturday night, and as usual, it would be complete with a roast pig, flower leis, and gallons of
punch that a group of hee-hawing guys always
spiked after nine o'clock. The Tri Betas were
co-hosts each year, so her attendance would be
mandatory.

"Can't wait," Courtney murmured to herself,
strolling toward the student union building. The
event was usually fun, but she knew the same old
people would be there, wearing their same old
Hawaiian shirts, making the same tame conver-

sation about the same old topics.

What's wrong with me? Courtney shook her head, as if to shake herself out of her mood. Quickly she checked her leather folder for the neat stack of rummage sale flyers Diane had produced on her desktop computer. She planned to post them in the student union cafeteria, bookstore, dining commons, and each dorm lounge. It was a simple design, but it was easy to read, Courtney thought sensibly.

She found a large bulletin board near the bookstore checkstands and began tacking a flyer in a prominent spot.

"Don't Miss the Tri Beta Rummage Sale— exclamation point," Courtney heard a voice behind her slowly reading the flyer.

She turned around, took a small step back, and wrapped her arms protectively about her leather folder. It was Dash Ramirez, investigative reporter for the U. of S. *Journal.* Courtney knew Dash through Lauren Turnbell-Smythe and admired his writing, even though she knew he was always trying to dig up dirt about sorority-fraternity life.

There was something about him, though, that put her a little on edge. His face was usually shadowed by a rugged, two-day stubble, and his blue jeans were so old they looked as if they were about to fall off his body.

"Hi, Dash," Courtney said pleasantly, making an effort to relax her grip on the folder. She slipped one hand into the pocket of her navy-blue skirt and looked curiously into his challenging black eyes, flashing with humor and intelligence. Something made her wonder what his real first name was. And where the nickname came from. She found herself staring at the way his dark hair curled a little over the collar of his faded denim shirt. "Brushing up on your reading skills?"

Dash grinned and held on to her gaze for a moment, as if he were deciding how best to respond. "Yes, I am. And thanks for the easy-to-read exercise." He slipped a flyer out of Courtney's hand and held it at arm's length, pretending to admire it. "In fact, it's stunning in its simplicity. A Tri Beta classic."

"Well?" Courtney said, refusing to let him fluster her. "You're in communications. Does it communicate our message clearly?"

"Wow," Dash said in a mocking voice, "does it ever."

Courtney felt the anger start to rise in her throat, but she was determined to face this cocky guy down. Dash was a classic case of insecurity frosted over with a thick, protective coating of sarcasm. She'd run into guys like him many times before.

"So, Dash," Courtney began, barely concealing the ice in her voice, "is there something more we can do to promote our rummage sale?"

"Well, in the first place," Dash began, "where do you sorority girls come off having a rummage sale? That's what middle-aged ladies in Kansas hold in their church basements. It's the most unoriginal fund-raising idea I can think of."

"Thanks."

"Well, you asked."

"Go on," Courtney said coolly, her heart beginning to swell with fury and indignation. Of course it was a lousy idea. Why was she even bothering to talk to him about it?

"Well, because you have such a dull idea," Dash sighed dramatically and shrugged, "publicity is going to be a real problem."

"Yes, I see," Courtney returned, her blazing blue eyes fixed on his face. "Many people—like you, for instance—require a great deal of hype in order to get them to do *anything*."

"You bet," Dash said thoughtfully. He snapped his fingers. "You've got it. Hype. That's the ticket. Sell the rummage sale with blatant hype, like the tacky department stores do."

Dash put his palms up in the air, as if he were reading something in the sky. "I can see it now. Have a plane write messages in the air. Dress up as clowns and pass out balloons when classes are letting out. Get boisterous. Obnoxious. Everyone will be so curious to know why the Tri Betas are behaving this way—they'll want to check out your sale."

Courtney felt her anger start to boil. She could tell her face was reddening and pinching up—and that Dash was loving it. "Oh, right, that sounds—"

"How about a van with a loudspeaker on top?" Dash interrupted her. "You could blare your message all over—"

"Oops, sorry," a girl carrying a tall stack of books said as she bumped into him accidentally.

Dash stopped and grinned. "Well, I think you get the general idea, Courtney. Hey, I have to take off. I have an editorial meeting that started five minutes ago. See you later." Dash gave her an exaggerated wink. "And let me know if you have any further promotional needs!"

Courtney opened her mouth to say something, but Dash was gone. She took a deep breath and tried to steady her angry, shaking chest. Who did he think he was, criticizing the rummage sale, her flyer, and her sorority—all in a few lighthearted, careless quips? Courtney angrily straightened up and headed for the cafeteria. Barely hearing the stream of familiar greetings thrown her way, she tossed her blond hair and pursed her lips tightly.

How dare he treat me like some ridiculous object, Courtney fumed silently, turning the corner into the cafeteria and colliding with a potted plant. The entire stack of blue and white flyers slipped out from under her arm and slid crazily across the floor.

"He's a punk," she muttered to herself, snatching the papers up from under a row of tables and chairs. "He's an obnoxious jerk who can't deal directly with anyone."

Courtney continued to steam, tapping the stack of disheveled papers on a tabletop. She turned and headed for the student lounge, where she flopped down on a soft couch and stared into space.

Her heart was still beating. Her face was tingling and flushed. She hadn't felt this alive in a long time. What was happening to her? Was she really angry at Dash? Or had his irreverent challenge stirred something in her? Something that—maybe—needed stirring?

Slowly, Courtney looked down at the dull-looking flyer. A small smile began to grow on her lips. She felt warm inside. What did she want, anyway? A guy who would fawn all over the terrible rummage sale idea, just like her Tri Beta sisters had?

Dash was different. He hadn't hesitated to confront her with the truth. He was funny and witty and challenging—everything that was missing from her Tri Beta sisters and the suitable preppie guys she always dated.

Courtney leaned her head back and smiled at the ceiling.

Dash was different, all right.

And difficult.

And handsome.

Something was happening.

Five

....

"Listen to this, Lauren," Winnie squealed, tapping her toes merrily on the dashboard of Lauren's Jeep as the two headed out for an afternoon of apartment hunting. "*Two bedroom executive townhouse with wall-to-wall carpeting, dishwasher, washer-dryer, mountain views, jacuzzi, pool. . . .* Give me a break! Hey, what's this? *Tsh comptr.* A computer, too?"

"Trash compactor," Lauren said, patiently flicking on her turn signal and heading out of the dorm parking lot. "My parents have one in their New York apartment. You put your garbage in it and it squishes it down tightly."

Winnie shook her head and watched as Lauren's Jeep rushed out through the ornate U. of S. entrance gate. Her blowup with Josh over their terrible living situation had made her stop and think. What they needed more than anything was a beautiful, peaceful place, all to themselves.

"I have to find a roomy apartment where Josh and I can really spread out," she told Lauren. "I promised Josh."

Yesterday Lauren had offered to take her apartment hunting. Winnie was grateful because Lauren knew everything there was to know about rental prices, utilities, deposits, and other mundane details. She'd even ordered Winnie to replace her glittery purple running pants and zebra-striped Lycra halter top with slacks and a plain white blouse so that she would look like a steady type for a prospective landlord.

Winnie stretched her long legs halfway out the rolled-down window and breathed in the cool spring air. She wished Josh were here with her. Apartment hunting was another new and wonderful adventure. Outside, Springfield's famous tall elms were leafing out and the roadway was dappled with sunlight.

"No way I'm getting an apartment with a trash compactor," Winnie thought out loud. "Josh would stick my precious junk in it."

"Plus, it's probably about eight or nine hundred dollars a month," Lauren noted, turning into an older neighborhood lined with mature shade trees.

Winnie's eyes opened wide. "You're kidding." She ducked her head back down in the Friday *Springfield Times* classified section and emerged with a stunned expression. "It *is* nine hundred dollars, Lauren. I don't believe it. Nine hundred dollars for well-crushed garbage. What's this world coming to?"

"Let's look at the apartment that's only four hundred dollars, Winnie," Lauren said sensibly. "You're going to have a lot of expenses living off campus. Expenses you never knew existed."

Winnie started to play nervously with her Looney Tunes earrings. "Actually, four hundred dollars sounds like a lot, too."

"Yeah, but it's in a good section of town close to campus, and it has closet space and a separate bedroom," Lauren replied. "It might be worth it."

Lauren turned right and cruised farther into the old neighborhood, her funky flowered blouse fluttering in the spring air. "It's nice here. You might be in luck."

"That would be good," Winnie said, unwrapping a large piece of bubble gum that she folded into her mouth. "Josh is pretty eager to settle somewhere. The electrical system had him so weirded out, he actually packed his entire computer system back over to the lab on campus. That's where he's been all day, trying to salvage the program he lost when our electricity went out."

"Happy Honeymoon," Lauren noted sympathetically.

"Oh, well," Winnie chattered on. "I'm so busy right now, I barely have enough time for my own life. But maybe that's the way it's going to be with me and Josh. We're always going to have busy, exciting lives—creating software programs, saving the sanity of college students . . ."

Lauren pulled over and studied her street map of Springfield.

"Besides, next to Mr. Angeletti's problems, mine are just small change," Winnie continued talking. "But he just checked into the U. of S. hospital to get some really fantastic experimental treatments for his lung cancer. In fact, I'm meeting KC and Faith there this afternoon to see him. *Then* I've got a shift at the Crisis Hotline.

Then I have to finish my Health Fair banners in time for tomorrow morning."

"Thank God tomorrow's Saturday." Lauren pulled out onto the road again and steered into a pleasant, shady neighborhood with tidy lawns and large, lovely homes. "I just finished a long piece for my creative writing class and I don't want to write another word for forty-eight hours. Oh, by the way, I'm going with Kimberly to the Health Fair tomorrow, so I'll get to see your banners."

"Great!" Winnie snapped her gum loudly.

Lauren pushed her wire-rimmed glasses up on her round face. "Kimberly's secret admirer left another letter, promising to reveal himself there."

"How romantic," Winnie said, silently making a note to herself. She was going to ask Josh to write her romantic notes. It would help keep the spark of their love alive. She could leave sexy replies under his pillow.

"Kimberly's nervous. So I told her I'd go along for moral support."

Winnie raised her eyebrows and giggled. "What will you do when their eyes lock together passionately on the gymnasium floor?"

Lauren smiled. "Hey, I'll do anything to get out of my dorm room."

A cloud passed briefly across Winnie's face. "Is Melissa doing any better? Has she talked to Brooks?"

Lauren shook her head in exasperation. "I don't think so," she said, searching the houses for street numbers. "But she won't talk to me, so I don't really know for sure."

"Superglue lips," Winnie said. Her fingers searched for the play button on Lauren's CD player. "Tell me about it. When she was *my* roommate, I could always sense when things were falling apart just by looking at her lips. Brooks was the only one who could crack them open."

"I feel so sorry for her," Lauren said softly. "Yesterday, she barely got out of bed. She actually missed track practice and skipped all of her classes. She just lies there, watching TV, eating ice cream, and pigging out on big stacks of cinnamon toast from the cafeteria."

Winnie slipped on a pair of hot-pink sunglasses and waved at a group of passing bicyclists in racing gear. "What is it with everyone these days? Just last night, Josh was actually yelling at me about the dumb utility shutoff. And now Mel is acting like losing Brooks is the end of the world. Well, it isn't!"

"Yeah, but . . ."

"She has to talk to someone soon," Winnie blared. "You can't just give in to depression, or it will suck you in."

Winnie flashed on the drills she'd learned at the Crisis Hotline.

Break the cycle. Get your depressed callers to do something different. They need a jolt. A swim. A laugh. An exotic dinner. Anything! The mildly depressed may only need a sudden change of perspective.

"How about surprising her with something?" Winnie suggested. "Rent an outrageous video, like the Three Stooges? Or bring her some sushi. Or a singing telegram."

Winnie broke off suddenly as they moved slowly past a perfectly restored, yellow-and-white Victorian home set back from the street. Surrounded by spreading trees and a lush green lawn, it was the most beautiful house Winnie had ever seen. Its wraparound front porch had a charming swing, and the front gate was framed with a trellised arch, thick with pink roses in full bloom. Her heart leapt when she saw a small sign in the window that read APT. FOR RENT.

"Lauren! Stop!" Winnie shrieked, unable to contain her ecstasy. "I've found the absolutely perfect place. It *has* to be available."

"But we're not quite there yet, Winnie." Lauren checked the number of the house. "The Alder Apartments aren't for another block or so."

Winnie twisted around in her seat. "It doesn't matter. Back up, Lauren, please! I've just found our apartment."

By the time Lauren had parked and locked the Jeep on the other side of the street, Winnie was already rushing up the front steps and ringing the doorbell. A young woman wearing jeans and carrying a towheaded baby on her hip answered the bell and took them upstairs.

Winnie's heart was beating wildly as she climbed the charming staircase to the third floor. The wooden banister was silky-smooth oak. The oriental rugs were soft and exotic. The house smelled of freshly baked bread.

"The cost of fixing up this old place got pretty steep," the woman explained. "So we decided to turn the attic into a studio apartment and rent it." She opened the apartment door with a key.

"Winnie!" Lauren whispered. "It's only a studio and it doesn't even have a separate entrance."

But Winnie barely heard what Lauren was saying. She was falling in love all over again. The low-ceilinged room was dominated by a large bay window, fitted with an upholstered window seat that overlooked the garden and babbling stream below. Although it was very small, it had new wall-to-wall carpeting and the walls had just been painted a soft white. The kitchen was tiny, but had cabinet doors with beveled-edge panes and quaint porcelain knobs.

Winnie gasped out loud when she saw the bathroom, barely large enough for her to stand up in, but fitted with an enormous claw-footed tub. It was the tub she'd always dreamed of having. Every night, she and Josh could have romantic, candlelit baths, just like they did their first night together as husband and wife.

"Where are the closets?" Lauren asked, inspecting the kitchen with a businesslike air.

"Uh, well, the closet is back here." The woman pushed the front door back to reveal a tiny, three-foot-deep enclosure.

"I'll take it," Winnie said, barely containing her ecstasy. "Oh, unless you need references and stuff like that. But, you see, my husband and I are very responsible people. Josh is getting his degree in computer science and I'm a psychology major and we're both doing very well and . . ."

The woman gave a friendly laugh. "You've

sold me. We've been looking for a nice married couple."

"Wait, Winnie," Lauren said, pulling her back. "You haven't even asked what the rent is—and whether the electrical system is adequate for—"

"It's five hundred and fifty dollars a month," the woman said. "We'll need your first month's rent upfront, plus a one-hundred-dollar damage deposit."

"Great," Winnie said, eagerly reaching for her purse.

"Winnie!" Lauren pressed her. "The rent is much more than the new one-bedroom we were going to look at. Are you sure?"

"It's fate, Lauren," Winnie said dreamily. "This apartment is everything I'd ever hoped for. Josh and I are going to be blissfully happy here. I just know it."

After dropping off a joyful Winnie at the U. of S. Hospital, Lauren slipped her shiny Jeep into traffic headed back to downtown Springfield. Helping Winnie find the apartment had boosted her spirits a little.

But Winnie wasn't her roommate. Melissa was. And Melissa was going to be three feet away from her in their tiny dorm room—pushing her away, shutting her out, making her feel like an intruder. Lauren didn't know how much more she could take.

What am I going to do if it doesn't work out? Pack up my boxes again? Drift into another shaky living situation with a complete stranger?

Melissa was the only solid roommate prospect she had on the entire campus. Melissa was the closest thing she had to her friendships with Winnie, Faith, KC, and Kimberly—friendships that had taken months to form. Friendships she'd never really had before. Maybe Winnie was right. Maybe she could do something to give Melissa a jolt.

Lauren parked the car in front of a Japanese restaurant. After picking up a foam container packed with three different kinds of sushi, she headed for the video store next door and picked out a stack of old movies. Driving back to Forest Hall, she had a heady sense that today things might be different with Melissa. After all, it had been nearly a week since the wedding debacle. Melissa was going to have to talk *sometime* to *someone*.

Carefully balancing the container of sushi on top of the videos, Lauren unlocked her dorm-room door and backed inside.

"Melissa?" she whispered. Everything was so quiet, Lauren assumed the room was deserted and flicked on the lights. But as she began unloading her packages, Lauren heard a sniffle and turned around.

Perched on her desk, staring out the window with her knees drawn up, was Melissa. Her red hair was plastered in strings against her forehead and her eyes were puffy from crying. Her baggy pajama top had been stuffed haphazardly into sweatpants.

"Melissa!" Lauren said. "I didn't think you were here."

Melissa lifted her balled-up fist away from her forehead long enough to turn and glance at Lauren. "Hi," she whispered, returning her gaze to the courtyard below.

Lauren climbed up on the opposite desk, pushed her books and papers aside, and crossed her slightly pudgy legs. She was determined to make a connection with Melissa.

"Look, Melissa," she began boldly. "I just want to say one thing. You don't think anyone understands what you're going through, but we do. There are a lot of people who care about you and want to help. Faith, KC, Winnie . . . they're all really worried about you."

"Thanks, Lauren," Melissa said, her stare glued to the window.

"How do you think I felt after breaking up with Dash?" Lauren persisted. "And when Dimitri turned out to be a total fake, I thought I'd never get over the humiliation. I was frightened. I thought my life wasn't worth living."

"Really?"

"Really. But I knew I had to do something to break out of my gloom, so I'm concentrating on what I love most to do—write." Lauren cautiously tiptoed toward her bag of goodies. "Now, you've got to pull yourself out of this bleak mood." She handed Melissa the container. "I brought you some sushi from that new Japanese restaurant on the Strand. How about trying some? It's supposed to be great. Or how about a movie? When was the last time you saw *E.T.*? I love the—"

"Are you serious?" Melissa snapped, turning her head around abruptly and throwing a wadded-up piece of tissue on the floor. "Just leave me alone."

There was a long silence. Lauren felt like she'd been punched in the stomach. Everything was slipping away. She'd have to move out. Campus authorities would shove her into another sterile dorm room.

"You don't know what you're talking about," Melissa suddenly burst out. "If you really knew what I was going through, you'd know that sushi won't make things better. *E.T.* won't make Brooks come back." She looked up, her green eyes blazing with sorrow. "Dash didn't promise his life to you, then desert you on the altar in front of your friends and family. Neither did Dimitri. How can you possibly compare yourself to *me*! You were *lucky* to get rid of that jerk Dimitri. And for all you know, you'll be back with Dash in no time."

"Melissa, *please*. I'm really sorry," Lauren said.

"Just go away!" Melissa wailed, sinking her head into her elbows, too exhausted to continue.

Lauren backed away and started to pick up her purse. Then she turned around and sat heavily back on her bed. Slowly, she reached for a book and lay down.

There wasn't anywhere else for her to go.

Six

The automatic front doors to the U. of S. Hospital flew open when KC reached the top of the building's concrete stairway. A blast of antiseptic-smelling air rushed past her, and for a brief moment KC wanted to run back across campus to the safety of her room.

In a few minutes, she would be meeting her father, who had driven from Jacksonville that morning with her mother and Grandma Rose to receive a new round of chemotherapy treatments.

It will be so good to see you again, Kahia, her

father had whispered to her over the phone the night before. *Save all your news for tomorrow. I want to hear everything about how well you're doing.*

KC steadied herself and took a deep breath.

How well I'm doing? I'm not well, Dad. In fact, everything is crazy. I tried to go back to my old life after I stopped taking the drugs. But nothing fits anymore. I don't know what I want. I don't know who Kahia Cayanne Angeletti is anymore. And I need your help.

Spotting a nurse seated at the front desk, KC stepped across the modern lobby, trying to breathe evenly and hold her head high. When she reached the shiny front counter, she straightened the shoulder strap on her purse, leaned forward, and cleared her throat. "Um, I'm meeting some-one receiving chemotherapy treatments here today," KC said. "What department is that?"

"Oncology. Outpatient treatment wing. Third floor," the nurse said abruptly, as if she said it a hundred times each day. She bent her head back down to a stack of papers.

"Thank you," KC whispered, moving slowly away.

This would be the first time she'd seen her father in several weeks, although she'd talked with him regularly on the phone. She never had the courage to ask anyone in her family how he looked. And now she wished she had.

"Would a member of the Thomas Daggett family please return to the surgery area?"

Cringing inwardly at the harsh voice on the hospital loudspeaker, KC turned and walked, dazed, toward a green elevator sign. Two nurses passed her, laughing. A bored-looking janitor emptied a garbage can into his cart.

KC pressed the third-floor button.

"Dr. Metropulos. Dr. Metropulos. Line 301 please. Line 301."

Winnie and Faith were waiting for her in the hall when she finally reached her father's room.

Faith stood up and smiled. Just seeing her familiar faded overalls and loose braid made KC feel a little better. "You're here," KC said, her eyes beginning to flood. "Thanks for coming."

"We'll see you through this," Faith said. "You're definitely not alone."

Winnie gave her a quick kiss. "It's going to be okay."

KC covered her face with her hands a moment and took a tissue Faith had quickly dug out of her purse. Then she took another deep breath and pushed open the door. Inside, she saw her father, half-hidden by a nurse taking her father's pulse.

"Dad? Mom?" KC whispered, peering into the dim room, wondering if he was asleep. The nurse looked up, smiled, and gathered her things, revealing her father, stretched out pale and thin on an adjustable hospital bed. A needle was taped to his arm and an IV bag hung silently above him. Her mother, knitting a nubby sweater at the foot of his bed, stood up and reached to embrace her.

"Hi, Mom," KC said quietly. "Dad?"

A chill went through KC's body as she drew closer, realizing how emaciated her father had become in such a short time. Even under his hospital gown, she could see that his once muscular legs were like two toothpicks. The burly arms that had once hugged her tight now lay thin and limp at his sides.

Nothing could have prepared her for this. Her insides were quaking, her hot tears were about to burst, and she felt on the verge of completely falling apart.

"Well, look who's here, Bud." Mrs. Angeletti gave KC an anxious smile and motioned for Faith and Winnie to come in.

Mr. Angeletti, who had been staring tiredly into space, looked over and smiled. Slowly, he lifted one arm and motioned to her.

"Kahia," he said, staring at her with unabashed tenderness. At least he was wearing his usual red bandanna around his head, with his shoulder-length, salt-and-pepper hair straggling out below, though his fuzzy beard had fallen out in large clumps. He lifted a strand of KC's hair. "My beautiful girl."

"Hi, Dad," KC whispered, barely able to breathe, realizing for the first time, in a blinding flash, how sick her father really was.

She sat down carefully on the edge of his bed. "How are you—feeling?"

Mr. Angeletti gave a quiet laugh and stroked her arm. "Aw, heck, I'm fine," he said. "If only these darn doctors would stay away, I'd be even better. But they want to poke and prod and play with their high-tech toys and drugs."

"But, Dad—"

"What I could really use," her father interrupted, "is two weeks on a nice hot Mexican beach."

"Oh, Bud," Mrs. Angeletti sighed, slipping her arm around his shoulders. "Be quiet."

"Winnie, you crazy woman, you," Mr. Angeletti said weakly, stopping every few words to take a breath. KC stared at the strange gray color in his face. "What did you go and get yourself married for? Can't you at least *live* with him first and find out if you can get along?"

Winnie moved forward and gave him a light hug. "We did what our hearts told us to do, Mr. Angeletti."

"You've met Josh, Mr. Angeletti," Faith spoke up. She perched tentatively on the edge of a chair. "He's a wonderful guy and Winnie's a lucky girl."

Mr. Angeletti smiled. "Yes, Mother Faith."

KC felt Faith's hand on her shoulder. "We just wanted to say hello," Faith whispered. "We'll leave you now."

"Hey," Mr. Angeletti strained. Winnie and Faith turned back. "Peace." He lifted one of his hands slowly and held up two fingers to make a V. Then he let his arm flop back down beside him.

KC's heart was breaking as she watched her mother quietly hug Faith and Winnie good-bye. Her face was haggard and there were thick sprouts of gray in her wavy red hair. Her ankles looked swollen over her worn Birkenstock sandals. Just by looking at her, KC understood how much she'd been going through, trying to take care of her dad and keeping the restaurant running.

"I brought some goat cheese and tomato sandwiches from The Windchime," her mother said, trying to sound cheerful. "Bite to eat, KC?"

"Okay, Mom," KC said in a daze, watching her father trying to catch his breath. His hands were shaking a little and KC saw that her father's brief visit with Faith and Winnie had completely sapped his strength. It was almost too much to bear. Before this illness, she'd never seen him sick before—or even tired.

"Your dad only has another round of chemo treatment later," her mother continued. "It really doesn't take long at all, KC. And it's such a nice drive from Jacksonville. Isn't it, darling?"

KC watched her father give her mom an understanding half smile. How could this have happened to him? KC thought bitterly. Cancer was something doctors discovered in stressed-out executives who ate fatty meats, drank, and smoked. Not in a man whose life's mission was to make sure everyone ate enough organically grown vegetables.

KC silently took the sandwich her mother offered her and pretended to take a bite.

"Where's Grandma Rose?" KC managed.

"She went to get a cup of coffee from the cafeteria. I'm going to meet her and see if she'd like to take a walk."

"Okay," KC said, though her throat was so tight she could barely speak. Why did her dad have to get sick now? Didn't anyone realize what was at stake? Her father was the strongest, wisest, most solid thing she could turn to. If she lost him now, before she got the answers she needed, she'd never figure out who she was—or what she was supposed to be doing with her life.

She stared intently at the crease in her pressed pants, terrified that her calm bedside manner would suddenly collapse into a raw display of tears and uncontrollable sobbing—just when her father needed her to be strong.

When she looked up, she saw that her father was looking at her, his twinkling blue eyes filled with love and concern. She heard her mother leave quietly through the door.

"Don't fight it, sweetheart," her father said, fumbling with a Kleenex box on his bedside table and handing her a tissue. "You can be sad."

KC grabbed the tissue and pressed it tightly to her eyes, sending a flood of hot tears down her cheeks that even the tissue couldn't contain. She pressed her toes into the linoleum floor and rocked back and forth soundlessly, unable to stop.

"I already know that you're strong, Kahia. You don't have to prove anything to me now."

"It's just that I didn't realize you'd . . ." KC was unable to continue and broke off into another chain of sobs.

Her father put his hand gently under her chin and lifted it. "Hey, baby. I know I don't look so good," he said haltingly. "They had me on some bad stuff at Jacksonville Memorial. Chemotherapy that made me pretty sick. I know I look like hell. But things are going to happen with this new treatment. Count on it."

KC lifted her eyes hopefully to her father's face.

"These research doctors," Mr. Angeletti continued, panting, "they know what they're doing."

"They do?"

Mr. Angeletti nodded his head and stroked his beard. "They've been slaving for years on a treatment that gets rid of my kind of tumor. It's real search-and-destroy stuff. I'm lucky to get it."

"I—wanted to tell you," KC gulped, "how sorry I am for the way I acted last fall."

Her father looked up, frowned, then smiled as

he remembered. He started to laugh, but the effort was too much for him. His breathing had become labored and he broke out into a coughing fit.

KC watched, horrified, as her father bent forward, unable to stop his deep, congested cough. "Oh, yes," Mr. Angeletti panted when the coughing stopped. "Parents weekend. The same weekend you—didn't want to see your parents."

"I didn't know how much it would hurt you, Dad," KC tried to explain. "Sometimes I forget that I'm not as separate from everything as I sometimes think I am. But I'm changing. I really am."

Mr. Angeletti gazed at her affectionately. "You must be growing up." There was a pause. "Aw, your two older brothers were the same way when they left home. But you see, Kahia. Fathers seem to think their daughters need them more."

"I thought I needed complete freedom from you," KC said earnestly, "so that I could break away and do what I needed to do. But—but now I know how much I need you."

"Freedom's just another word for nothing left to lose," her father cracked out a barely audible melody. "Yeah," he whispered, tiredly touching his forehead with a trembling hand.

KC knew that she should let her father rest. But she had a quickening sense that now was the time to talk. Would she ever have the chance again? She was aching to confess her recent experiment with drugs because she knew he would understand. And maybe he could tell her what was behind the unfamiliar, haunting feeling she had now—a feeling that she no longer knew who she was.

KC slid carefully over to her father's bed and took his hand.

"Oh, no," her father breathed, "it's that intense Kahia look we—all—know so well."

"I've got to talk to you."

"Kahia," he said gently. "Next week. I can't talk with this damn needle in my arm."

"But, Dad," KC couldn't help herself, "I'm so confused."

"I can tell." Mr. Angeletti stroked her hand, struggling to breathe. "Listen—we have plenty of time. Tell me your secrets next week and don't look at me like I'm about to drop dead, because I'm not."

"Dad . . ."

"We have all the time in the world to talk," her father wheezed. "Maybe even I have a few secrets to confess. But when the time is right."

KC's heart stopped. "What secrets?"

"Hey, when the doc tells me my days are numbered, we'll talk." Mr. Angeletti closed his eyes and KC stared numbly down at the tiny pattern in his hospital gown.

"Talk about what?"

"Ah, that's my secret to keep until I'm ready, sweetheart." Mr. Angeletti opened his eyes briefly. "Now you let me take a little nap so I can get this over with and go home."

KC sat quietly and looked at her father's thin face on the pillow. Inside, her mind was racing wildly. What was he talking about? What secret? Had the doctors given him some weird medication that made him say things? The father she knew never kept secrets from his family.

Outside the room, in the hallway, she could hear the continuous sounds of rattling food trays, intercom announcements, and gurneys thundering by. It seemed as if life were going on everywhere but in the bare hospital room where she sat with her father. It was as if she'd been put into a dark box, and only her father had the key that would unlock it.

It's impossible that anything could happen to him now, she thought. *Impossible.*

Seven

Next time you take it upon yourself to improve on *Dungeons and Dragons*, young man, make sure you've got adequate power. This is basic stuff, Mr. Gaffey. I'll give you one week to complete the program. If it's not done by then, you will receive a failing grade for the assignment.

The light was beginning to fade as Josh headed quickly across the dorm green that afternoon toward the edge of campus. After staring at his computer screen for three straight hours, his eyes felt like two desert rocks and there was a stabbing pain in the back of his neck.

Still, Josh had a bleary sense of relief. That afternoon, he'd gone directly from his Computer Science 301 class to the lab, where his memory had clicked into blissful autopilot. Even though Dr. Atkins had chewed him out for not having his program turned in on time, he felt sure now that he'd be able to re-create it by the middle of next week.

As he passed Forest Hall, he waved briefly to a group of his old dorm buddies headed toward the warm light streaming out of the dining commons. For a brief moment, he was tempted to stop them. His stomach was growling, and he realized he hadn't eaten since morning. Maybe they could load up a plate for him and slip it out.

Instead, Josh dug his hands deep into his jeans pockets and turned sharply onto the path that led off-campus. Winnie was packing their stuff for tomorrow's move, and she could probably use his help now. Anyway, he was anxious to find out what kind of a place she'd found for them to live in. It would be enough of an event to celebrate over a hamburger dinner for two at the Big Burg Drive In.

Josh dug his thumbs into the straps of his bookbag and broke out into a light jog. He didn't particularly like the grim, run-down neighborhood they were staying in, but he'd been a military brat long enough to know that the place itself didn't make the home. Home was about people living their lives together. And now he was living it with Winnie.

Warm, loving, quirky Winnie, Josh thought happily, jumping over a gutter and racing across a busy crosswalk. He'd give up a thousand Salisbury steak dinners in the dining commons for one too-expensive burger with her. Over and over, his wedding vows repeated themselves in his mind.

For richer or poorer, in sickness and in health, till death do us part.

He and Winnie had made this promise to each other—this incredible, unbelievable promise. It made him feel strong and weak all at the same time.

When he finally reached their ancient brick apartment building, he was more anxious than ever to see her. He burst through the kicked-in front door and began rushing eagerly up the staircase.

"Now just you wait a minute, young man," Josh heard Mrs. Calvin's sharp voice behind him. He stopped and looked down at a thin woman wearing a nylon turban and a drab housecoat.

Josh stared at her, trying to look respectable. "Hello."

"Your wife or whoever she really is up there on the fourth floor has been warned that she has to move her things out by tonight," the landlady said, looking at him suspiciously. "I've got a man coming in at noon tomorrow and she's not making much progress. *That* I can tell you."

"Yes, well, my *wife* and I are planning to move first thing tomorrow morning," Josh explained.

"MMMMmmmm." Mrs. Calvin looked Josh up and down. "Leave the key on the kitchen counter when you go."

After she'd closed the door, Josh trudged up the staircase, deciding the building smelled like a sickening combination of sour milk, old dogs, and week-old tuna-fish sandwiches. He slipped the key into the door of the apartment, hoping Winnie had gotten a head start on their big packing job.

He stopped cold in the doorway when he saw her.

Surrounded by dozens of flickering candles was Winnie, still touching up the Health Fair banner that now spanned the entire length of the tiny apartment. To make room for it, Winnie had haphazardly stacked all of their collapsing cardboard boxes into a far corner. Piles of dirty laundry were hanging out of book boxes, notebooks were squashed against the wall, and clumps of paint-smeared rags were scattered all over the kitchen floor.

"Josh!" Winnie looked up at him with a dazzling smile. Her zebra-striped, leotard-clad legs were sprawled out behind her and her head was covered with a funky 1950s-style net. "You're here! How did your program go? Can you believe how big these banners are getting? I'm trying to finish them up, so I can get over to the hotline for my late shift."

Josh stared at her as she continued to happily relate the events of the day. For an instant, she reminded him of a little girl whose Daddy was picking her up at nursery school. His neck was gradually tensing up again.

"I had the greatest visit with Mr. Angeletti at the U. of S. Hospital this afternoon, Josh," Winnie continued blithely on. "He was getting his treatment, but he was so great. He teased me about getting married so young. Josh—I just know he's going to get better."

"Win . . ." Josh started, his heart sinking.

Hadn't she looked for an apartment like she said she would?

"Anyway," Winnie interrupted. "When are you going to buy that old station wagon of Mikoto's? I've been thinking about it because I'm going to need it to deliver these banners to the Health Fair."

Josh felt his neck get hot. He suddenly realized that his jaw was clenched tightly and that the hands in his pockets had balled up into two rock-like fists. The apartment was still a total disaster area.

Then he remembered. He and Winnie were together. They had to work things out. There was no reason to get all worked up about a bunch of junk. He knew Winnie wasn't the neatest person in the world when they got married. Slowly, consciously, he relaxed his hands.

Winnie continued to make yellow butterfly shapes around the word "JOY." "Do you think the station wagon has enough room?"

"Win, I'm still trying to get my head above water with that program that's due," Josh said, trying to act calm. "I've been at the computer lab all day and haven't had a chance to look at the wagon."

Winnie looked up. "You haven't?"

"Well, no, Win," Josh began. "You know that I lost hours of work last night when the power went off."

"Yes, but I'm never going to be able to carry these banners over," Winnie said, sighing and returning to her butterflies.

Josh's neck was tensing up again. He thrust his hands into his jeans pockets. Did she still want him to do everything? Who did she think he was? Her slave? "We'll have to get the car checked out first, anyway," Josh said, trying to sound patient.

"Okay, okay." Winnie rolled her eyes.

Josh gulped and looked at the mountains of junk surrounding Winnie and her banners. He couldn't even get to the bathroom if he needed to.

Rage began to sink slowly into every pore of his body. "Winnie?"

"What?" she said distractedly.

"Winnie?" Josh repeated, unable to control the shaking in his voice. "What are you *doing*?"

Winnie's eyes opened wide and she sat up on her heels, looking frightened to the tips of her bright orange fingernails. "I'm finishing my banners."

"Is that all you can think about?" Josh burst

out, throwing his backpack down. "You've been working on those banners for nearly a week now, and we're still not ready to move. Heck! We don't even *have* anywhere to go! Except the street, of course. And that's exactly where we're headed because Mrs. Calvin isn't about to give us a grace period. Is this registering?! Look at all of this useless junk you've trashed all over the place! There's paint everywhere and there's no way we're going to be out of here in time!"

"But, Josh . . ." Winnie began, then broke off. Josh could see her face crumple and her eyes begin to fill with tears. With his back to the wall, he sank slowly down until he was crouched on his heels, staring forlornly at the chaotic mess. He told himself to get a grip, but inside, he was flailing around like a drowning man. Would their whole life together be like this—moving from one dump to the next—forever getting their wires crossed and their priorities mixed up?

"Josh . . ." Winnie began to move toward him.

"And how can you be so unrealistic about Mr. Angeletti?" Josh barked back, hardly recognizing the mean, bitter sound of his voice. "Why do you think they're treating him at the U. of S. Hospital with their extreme, experimental drugs?

It's because they're desperate! Get real, Winnie. Face it. He's in bad shape!"

Slowly, Winnie drew herself up and looked down at him with burning eyes. Josh had never seen her look like that, as if all of the humor and sweetness had been drained out of her face forever. There was a painful silence as she proudly picked her way to the kitchen counter and came back with two keys dangling from her finger.

Her eyes continuing to pour hot lava, Winnie thrust one of the keys and a slip of paper in his face. "Here."

"Here what?"

"It's the key to our apartment."

"The key to our . . ." Josh looked at it, stunned. "You found an apartment?"

Winnie began tearfully gathering her things together. "You somehow *think*, Josh, that you're the only one taking responsibility around here. But *I'm* the one who found the place where we've been living for *free* all this week and *I'm* the one who found us an apartment."

Winnie darted into the bathroom and yanked a line of toilet paper off the roll, blowing her nose noisily into it. "I'm leaving for my hotline shift. Look at the apartment yourself. The one thing I ask of *you*, Josh Gaffey, is to buy the stupid station wagon and take my banners to the Health Fair tomorrow by nine A.M. After that, I won't ask a thing of you again in my *life*."

His chin sinking to his chest, Josh watched her grab the doorknob and jerk the door open. Then she stopped, looked back at him, and narrowed her eyes. "And don't *ever* talk that way about Mr. Angeletti again. He's going to survive. And—and I love—him very—much." She slammed the door loudly and Josh could hear her sobbing down three flights of stairs until the front door closed with a thump.

Josh rose and stared miserably at Winnie's JOY poster. Then he carefully blew out her candles. There was no way he was going to stand around in this smelly apartment, surrounded by Winnie's junk.

He looked at the crumpled slip of paper Winnie had handed him. The apartment's address was printed on it neatly and he realized that it was only about ten blocks away. Stuffing the key into his jeans pocket, Josh headed downstairs and into the night.

He continued walking until the avenue moved into a nicer neighborhood with tall shade trees. His spirits lifted as he looked into the brightly lit windows of the large, old homes lining the street. Growing up on military bases, he'd always longed to live in a neighborhood like this, where families actually settled down and never had to move.

Finally, he reached an elaborate yellow-and-white Victorian house whose street number matched the one on the slip of paper. After introducing himself to the landlady, he climbed the stairway and let himself into his new home.

When he peered inside, his heart sank.

The apartment was only a small studio, barely large enough for him to stretch out in. There would be no separate room for him to use when he needed a quiet place to study, and zero closets for Winnie to store her boxes of junk. Josh turned into the bathroom, banging his head on the low door frame. To his horror, he saw that there was no shower—only an oversized bathtub that barely left enough room for someone to brush their teeth.

Panicked, Josh quickly inspected the electrical outlets. All of them were aging, two-pronged plates, one of them falling off the wall, so that he could see the ancient, frayed, fabric-covered wiring. There was no way the system could handle his computer, even if he could plug it in.

"How could she do this?" he muttered.

"Doesn't she understand that I need a place to work?"

Josh sat down numbly at the quaint Victorian table next to the window, not knowing whether to laugh or check into the nearest mental hospital. The apartment was a disaster. He'd have to practically live at the computer lab to get his work done.

Then a slip of paper caught his eye, and Josh felt suddenly sick. It was the landlord's receipt. Winnie had agreed to rent it for an astronomical five hundred and fifty dollars a month. More, he knew, than they could easily afford.

His only thought now was to get back to his old room in the dorm, where he could crash and pretend things were normal again. He wanted nothing more than to put his brain in reverse and become an ordinary eighteen-year-old single college student again: hanging out with his buddies; nerding out at the Zero Bagel.

He'd take care of buying Mikoto's station wagon, but after that—forget everything.

Rushing down the carpeted stairway, Josh nearly crashed into the landlady, who was carrying her baby out of the bathroom.

"How do you like it?" she called out. "I know you'll be really happy . . ."

Josh tried to give her a friendly wave, but was

out the ornate front door before she could even finish her sentence. Running through the dark night, all Josh could think of was getting over to the dorms. After sprinting across the campus green, his sneakers were soaked and he was breathing hard. But at least he'd run off the worst of his anger.

"Hey, dude," a thin guy wearing a T-shirt and a pair of bright suspenders said as Josh pushed through the early stages of Forest Hall's usual Friday night blowout. An indoor volleyball net had been set up near the dorm entrance and a large group of athletic types were sprawled out, tossing a basketball back and forth. Loud music blared from a stack of speakers in the corner. "There's a rumor going around that you got married," the guy said with an incredulous look. "What's going on, man?"

"Hey, Dante." Josh held his hand up and the thin guy slapped it down. Dante was a drama-major friend of Faith's he didn't particularly like. But Josh spread a fake grin all over his face. Admitting defeat in front of all these guys would just make him feel worse. "All of it's true," he said. "My beautiful bride is working tonight and I just stopped by to take Mikoto's station wagon off his hands."

Dante stared at Josh and nodded his head up and down absently. "Not going to waste any time slipping into that suburban life-style, huh?" Dante joked. "Hey! Next week, we'll be hearing that you took on a mortgage. Next month, you'll have a family on the way, you son of a gun, you."

Josh felt his stomach tighten as Dante went on.

"Listen." Dante leaned his head next to Josh's. "Peter Dvorsky's Yamaha is in the basement at Coleridge Hall. He didn't have time to sell it before he took off for Europe, so he asked me to. Only three hundred. Now that would make your married life interesting."

Josh's ears perked up. He'd always dreamed of owning a motorcycle. Of flying across the Arizona desert; of exploring the Rockies; of taking a road north to Canada and seeing how far he could go. His life wasn't only going to be about computers, school, and Winnie. There had to be a place for adventure, too. Winnie knew that. Didn't she? "Can I see it?" he asked, offhandedly catching a basketball flying through the air.

"Sure," Dante said, grinning. "It's a beauty."

Josh bopped the basketball back and forth

between his hands, then threw it back into the noisy crowd. "Let's take a look," he said casually, opening the door with a flourish. Before he knew it, he was following Dante to the Coleridge Hall basement and watching him unlock a caged area where Peter's shiny motorcycle stood gleaming in the dim light, leaning provocatively to the side.

"It's a beaut, all right," Josh said, running his hand along the seat. Unable to resist, he slung one leg over and sat down on the springy leather. He gripped the wide-spaced handlebars and felt the heft of the machine. It was a good bike with plenty of power, capable of making long-distance trips. He knew how much it had meant to Peter, and how scrupulously he had taken care of it. Three hundred dollars was a bargain.

What am I thinking of? Josh thought to himself. *Winnie and I don't need a bike to buzz around in. We need a practical car to carry practical stuff in.*

Josh twirled the tiny earring in his left ear. His mind was racing. Winnie had blown six hundred and fifty dollars on an overpriced, impractical closet without even checking to see if it could handle his computer. That wasn't being very responsible and practical. Why did he need to be?

Josh shrugged his shoulders nervously and looked at Dante, who gave him a challenging stare. Maybe Dante was right. A motorcycle *would* make married life interesting. They'd find a way to move their stuff. And Winnie might even love the idea. Anyway, Josh concluded, they weren't going to do *everything* Winnie's way.

It was his life, too.

"I'll take it," Josh said, pulling out his wallet and taking out three one-hundred-dollar bills. "I won't even bargain with you, Dante. I know the bike is worth at least that."

"Deal," Dante said, nodding with approval.

Together they rolled the bike into a utility elevator and out through the dorm's service entrance.

Turning on the powerful engine, Josh waved at Dante. "Take it easy," he shouted before speeding off down the wooded street toward the Zero Bagel.

The night air was wild in his hair, and at least for a moment, Josh forgot everything else.

Eight

"One! Two! And one! Two! And one! Two!" a perky blond girl in a glittering lavender leotard was shouting from the Health Fair's giant center stage.

It was five minutes before ten o'clock on Saturday. Kimberly and Lauren had just stepped onto the converted U. of S. basketball court, and were surveying the fair's extravagant display of multicolored banners, balloons, and booths.

Five minutes. In five minutes, I'll know who he is, Kimberly told herself silently. *In five minutes, he won't be a secret admirer any longer. He'll be a live person I can actually talk to.* She sighed nervously. *Life's about to get very interesting.*

The loud aerobics music was throbbing in Kimberly's ears and she instinctively began swaying her hips to the beat. Still, she was too excited to give the huge exercise dance act more than a passing glance. She checked her watch again.

Nine fifty-six.

"What in the world are they doing?" Lauren murmured, tilting her head to the side.

"It's called step aerobics," Kimberly said absently, her eyes searching for directions to the Environmental Science exhibition area, where her rendezvous was supposed to take place. "They burn up lots of calories stepping up and down on those platforms to the music. It can be lots of fun with a good instructor."

Lauren shrugged, looking down at her own slightly generous thighs. "Maybe I should try it. I bet the instructor doesn't have an ounce of fat on her legs."

"You bet," Kimberly agreed, grabbing Lauren's elbow and dragging her along past a video on Red Cross lifesaving techniques. "Once you get in shape you burn fat like crazy. If you did that for six months you'd be laughing. Ice cream every night. Midnight pig outs. You wouldn't gain an ounce."

"Really?" Lauren looked serious.

Kimberly checked her watch again.

Nine fifty-seven.

"Come on, you innocent, you." Kimberly did an exaggerated roll of the eyes and continued to drag her friend through the crowd.

Then Kimberly spotted a bold sign hanging from the ceiling that read *Health Fair '92— Environmental Sciences Area!* Her heart beating faster and her legs feeling heavier by the second, she began rapidly inventing mental pictures of Sam or James wearing the giveaway cowboy hat and yellow rose.

Sam was the most likely candidate, Kimberly thought nervously, since he already wore western-style shirts and blue jeans to class. On the other hand, James had been more attentive to her in the last week. And although she couldn't quite imagine him in a Texas-style get-up, she *could* imagine him going to the trouble of finding out where her home was. James was more romantic than . . .

"Like to taste Sunny Hill's Fresh Plump Strawberry Yogurt?" a girl dressed up as a strawberry asked, moving a tray toward Kimberly and

Lauren. "It's locally made and contains no artificial anything!"

Kimberly shook her head, and for a heart-gripping instant, she caught a glimpse of a cowboy hat near a safe sex display.

"I'll try some," Lauren said. She hung back, taking a small sample cup, just as a guy in jeans and a sweatshirt stumbled into her.

"HHHEEEELLLP!" the guy gasped, gripping his chest and crumpling to the gym floor as Kimberly and Lauren looked on, horrified.

"Someone call a doctor!" Kimberly yelled, just as the stricken guy looked up at her and winked. A group of white-coated students from the medical school rushed through to demonstrate CPR techniques on the guy staging the faked heart attack.

Her heart still pounding in her ears, Kimberly slowly stood up and looked around, more anxious than ever and too pinned in by the crush of bodies to move an inch.

Nine fifty-nine.

Grabbing Lauren's arm, Kimberly inched her way out of the crowd, desperately hoping that she wasn't too late to meet her secret admirer.

"That scared me to death!" Lauren gasped, half laughing. "*I* almost had a heart attack just looking at him. What's the matter? Are we late?"

Kimberly nervously tugged at the scarf pulled through the belt loops of her form-fitting blue jeans. She was half-tempted to run out of the crowded fair, jog back to her room, and bury herself under her quilt. Her secret admirer's nerve-racking buildup was starting to give her a bad case of stage fright. What would she say to him when she finally did meet him? What if she blurted out something dumb and blew the whole dramatic moment? What was *he* going to do? Kiss her? Proclaim his love for her in an embarrassing display right in front of the entire Health Fair?

"I don't know," Kimberly stammered. "I thought I saw a cowboy hat before that guy pulled the stunt on us—but now I don't see anything."

Lauren narrowed her eyebrows. "Where? Where did you see him? Come on!"

Ten o'clock.

"No, let's go," Kimberly said, looking up from her watch and stepping back. "This is crazy. It was a fun game for a while, but I don't like it anymore. I feel too self-conscious."

Lauren's arms lay limply at her sides.

"Kimberly! Don't panic. You've been looking forward to this for a long time."

Suddenly, Kimberly's hand went out in front of Lauren. Her heart stopped beating and there was a heavy lump of dread in her throat. Across the room, standing next to an air-quality analysis display, was a guy with a large cowboy hat perched jauntily on his head. A single yellow rose was fixed to the lapel of his too-large jacket.

It wasn't sultry Sam Howard.

It wasn't handsome James Ryder.

It was Clifford Bronton.

Unable to speak or move, and her heart sinking by the second, Kimberly stared numbly at Clifford's pudgy, short profile. After all of the excitement over the flowers and the beautiful notes and the possibility of an exciting romance—Clifford Bronton? Nice, short, funny Clifford who sat behind her in lab? Who pretended to be a nice, unthreatening friend she could relax and joke around with? Who was about as sexy as a big brown teddy bear?

Just then, Clifford began to move away from the display. His head quickly turned and his eyes wandered in Kimberly's direction. Panicked, Kimberly darted her eyes away, pretending she didn't see him. She stepped back and whirled around in the direction of the gymnasium exit, nearly crashing into a booth demonstrating a body-fat pinch test.

"Kimberly!" she could hear Lauren shouting. "Where are you going?"

But Kimberly couldn't stop running, feeling more ashamed of herself with each step. Why couldn't she have said hello? Why couldn't she have just smoothed it over graciously like anyone else? Why was she acting like a third-grader? What if he'd seen her? Facing him again would be impossible.

When she reached the door, her face was as hot as fire and Lauren was still chasing her.

"Kimberly!" Lauren panted. "What happened back there? Did you see him?"

Turning to face her, Kimberly felt her eyes begin to burn. "It—it wasn't who I thought it would be. And—and I ran away like a complete idiot."

Lauren reached out with a sympathetic hand. "You're blowing this thing way out of proportion."

"I know! I know!" Kimberly cried out, pulling away from Lauren and running out the door. Lauren was right. She was freaking out just like she had over every other performance in her life. The anticipation had gotten to her, and now she'd made a fool of herself over none other than short, dumpy Clifford Bronton.

She'd never forgive him for this. Never.

Dash Ramirez was feeling restless. For the last hour, he'd been checking out the Health Fair, interviewing a bland collection of nutritionists, exercise nuts, and medical experts. It wasn't his idea of great investigative journalism, but he owed one to his editor, Greg Sukamaki. Since he'd broken off with Lauren, he hadn't exactly been a ball of fire for the *Journal*. Besides, if he could think of an angle, it might make a decent story.

Spotting a bank of empty bleachers, Dash flicked his narrow reporter's notebook shut and loped up to the top row. Maybe something catchy would pop into his brain up there, away from the milling crowd of crazed health nuts.

Still, he thought, stretching his bleach-stained jeans in front of him, something was bugging him. And, as much as he hated to admit it to himself, he knew what had set him off.

It was Courtney Conner.

Beautiful, cool, in-control Courtney Conner. He'd teased her a little yesterday at the bookstore. After all, he knew her slightly, from when she helped him dig up information about Lauren's last boyfriend, track-star fraud Dimitri Costigan Broder. She seemed too smart for the predictable sorority scene, but what did he know, anyway?

Dash shrugged. Maybe Courtney had all the answers. She looked like the type who knew what she wanted and went after it.

He didn't, that was for sure.

Dash stared dully down at aerobics dancers and tried to entertain himself with the Ridiculous Headlines Game he and Lauren had invented together.

Local Aerobics Instructor Actually Ground-breaking University Robot Project! he began lamely before thoughts of Lauren distracted him.

A few moments before, Dash had spotted Lauren with a friend strolling toward the entrance to the fair. Now he couldn't get her out of his mind. If Lauren were with him, she would have dug up a great angle by now. And she would have collected some unbelievable quotes, too. That was the thing about Lauren. People took one look at her soft, violet eyes, her innocent, round face, and they'd tell her anything.

Dash sank his forehead into one of his hands. It was impossible for him to be without her. Sure, it had been his fault the relationship had ended. He'd been furious the night she publicly humiliated him, claiming he was trying to take full credit for their joint university Regent's award for investigative journalism.

But that was weeks ago. He'd had time to think about his fat head since then. And now he wanted her back.

Just tell me what I have to do, Lauren, he thought.

Then Dash remembered his column in the *Journal.* It had just come out, and he'd torn it out of the morning paper. It was one of the best pieces he'd ever written—and it was about Lauren. About breaking up. About all the things he'd never told her.

Now all he needed to do was pull it out of his back pocket and hand it to her. She'd understand that the words were meant for her—that they were words he couldn't tell her to her face.

He looked up and gazed out at the crowd, suddenly seeing a new girl on the *Journal* staff waving at him from the bottom of the bleachers.

What was her name? Amanda? Amelia?

"When are we going to talk about that rock column?" she called out, smiling suggestively. "Let's get together!"

Dash flashed a grin. "Sure, sure!"

He stroked his two-day stubble and tried to imagine Lauren swaggering up to a guy she barely knew and suggesting that they "get together." Maybe Courtney would, in a classy way. But Lauren? Never.

Quiet, unassuming, soft-spoken Lauren. Didn't she understand how he felt about her?

As he scanned the crowd, he suddenly saw the unmistakably wispy outline of Lauren's hair. She was standing by herself, watching an acupuncture demonstration through her steel-rimmed glasses. Dash was beginning to feel nervous and shy just looking at her soft hair and the gentle way her denim dress hung on her body. He loved the curious way she looked at things, as if she were seeing something no one else could.

His heart doing double time, Dash headed down the bleachers toward her. He could feel his hands get shaky. What was he scared of? Scared that their relationship was over for good? Scared that she would say nothing?

"Hi," Dash said, strolling up casually to her.

"Planning on getting punctured yourself?"

He watched her beautiful eyes turn toward him. Her face softened a little, but her round mouth was tensing up the way it always did when she was nervous.

"Hi, Dash. Needles look a little scary to me," Lauren answered. She looked down at his shoe and bit the corner of her bottom lip.

Why couldn't she come right out and say, *I miss you, Dash. Can we give it another try?*

That's all it would take. Didn't she know that he was in no shape to take charge of this situation? All he wanted to do was wrap his arms around her and get her out of this obnoxious place.

"Hey." Dash nervously grabbed the column in his back pocket, not knowing what to say next. "I thought you'd like to see this."

Lauren raised her eyebrows anxiously. "Oh. Thanks," she said, taking the clipping gingerly out of his hand. She barely glanced at it before folding it up and sticking it into her purse.

"So, how's everything?" Dash asked, desperately trying to hide the tremor in his voice. With Lauren so near, it was hard for him to think of anything intelligent to say. All he could do was stare at her eyes, the familiar curve of her lips, the dress she wore the day they found out they'd won their investigative journalism award.

"Fine. Fine," Lauren replied, nodding and snapping her purse shut. Slowly, she began backing away, as if she wanted to leave.

"Great. Guess I'll see you around," Dash answered, slowly raising one hand up in a feeble salute.

"Yeah. Nice to see you," Lauren said softly.

"Uh, yeah, right. Enjoy the fair," Dash mumbled, his heart sinking like lead as he stared at Lauren's back disappearing into the noisy crowd. At this rate, he'd get to have a full-length conversation with Lauren by next Christmas. It was hopeless. He'd never meet anyone who meant as much to him as Lauren did.

But that's just the way it was between men and women. Two steps forward, three steps back. An endless, useless game that wasted everyone's time and energy. No one ever had the guts to come right out and say what they felt.

And he was as guilty as anyone.

Nine

"You can never be too careful these days," Marcia Tabbert pointed out, sliding her chair out from Tri Beta's glossy mahogany meeting table that morning. Her delicate forehead wrinkled prettily under her pink velvet headband. "When you date a fraternity guy, at least you know what you're getting into."

Courtney took a sip of her iced tea and found herself slipping into her familiar half-awake state. She didn't have to really listen to Marcia's words. She knew in advance what the script called for.

"That's not necessarily so," Annette Champlain spoke up, tilting her head in gentle disagreement, revealing a tasteful pearl earring.

Ah-ha. A disagreement! Courtney smiled inwardly, half-ashamed of her impatience. After all, these were her friends and sisters. What was wrong with her?

"Susan Brooks met her boyfriend at a dorm party during rush week and he's really nice: pre-law and from a really good family in Seattle," Annette continued. "She's getting him to join Sigma Chi though, so they'll have more activities in common."

At least I didn't know what Dash Ramirez was going to say next, Courtney suddenly thought, a chill going up her spine.

"For God's sake, there *are* other things to do on this huge campus besides going to Greek parties, you know," Diane Woo objected, running her smooth nails through her glossy black hair. "Believe it or not, ladies, there are concerts, plays, sports events, dorm parties, private parties—all out there waiting for anyone looking for a little fun and diversity."

"Snore," freshman Sarah Mills tossed back. "Everyone knows that all the really important parties are Greek. And where else can you get dressed up and go to a party with people who are really—going places?"

Courtney smiled to herself. *Dash Ramirez would die of laughter listening to us right now,* she thought. *Or maybe he'd understand. Who knows? Maybe he's a lot more understanding than he shows. But how will I ever know?*

Diane sat back in her chair, exasperated. "Just last night, I went to a great party with my Renaissance history seminar group at Dr. Edwards's house . . ."

"Oh, give me a break, Diane!" Marcia burst out. "That sounds totally boring!"

Diane smiled mysteriously. "Marcia, the gorgeous graduate student I met was definitely not boring. And if I didn't have this Phi Delta thing tonight, I'd be meeting him downtown for an exotic Greek dinner, followed by an incredibly sexy French film at the University Exit Theater."

Everyone laughed, including Courtney, who took a long, cool drink of her iced tea and stared out the window to the manicured lawn sloping away from the terrace.

She found herself daydreaming about a romantic date with Dash, curled up on an old café chair wearing nothing but a pair of faded jeans and a baggy sweater. For hours, they'd argue intensely about none other than a sexy French film they'd just seen. Then something in his flashing black eyes would stop her. His hand would slide across the table into hers. Slowly, his rugged, handsome face would draw close to hers. Their lips would meet . . .

"Courtney?" Diane was saying. "Earth to Courtney!"

Courtney looked up at the table of pleasant Tri Beta faces that had grown silent, waiting for her to say something. "What? I—I'm sorry."

"You dated a guy from the dorms last fall, Courtney," Diane pressed her. "You don't regret it, do you?"

Courtney felt her lips take on a warm smile. "No. Phoenix was great."

Stephanie leaned forward earnestly. "But, Courtney, you only dated him for a few weeks."

"He was just a plaything for you anyway, Courtney," Marcia drawled. "I couldn't believe the way he showed up here with his long hair and tie-dyed shirts."

Courtney shrugged and fingered her antique wristwatch. Her soft blond hair fell forward and tickled her cheeks. Then there was Dash Ramirez. He was different, but he was no laid-back innocent. Unlike Phoenix, he'd have plenty to say if she took him on her usual round of frat parties and academic lectures.

Her cheeks got warm just thinking about their last encounter outside the U. of S. bookstore. He'd been bold. He'd been funny. He'd pounced on the silly rummage sale like a tomcat and for once, she'd been easy prey. Why did she find this feeling so deliciously exciting?

"Courtney!" Diane nudged her. "You are completely out of it. What are you smiling about?"

Courtney looked up and saw that the rest of the girls were drifting out of the meeting, leaving her practically alone in the elegant room. A few shiny heads of hair turned back and gave her questioning looks. She felt light-headed and giddy, as if she were being filled with a strange energy that had nowhere to go.

"Nothing," Courtney said softly. Suddenly, everything about Dash was in sharp focus. The flashing black of his eyes. The intensely naked feeling she had with him, as if he had X-ray vision into her mind. He was all danger and unpredictability—and she suddenly wanted nothing more than to be close to it.

"Come on," Diane urged. "Let's get dressed for the luau."

"Yes," Courtney said absently. Dash Ramirez. Dash Ramirez. She had to talk to him. If she didn't do something fast, she'd lose her mind. Where did he live? Did he have a phone? What would he say? What could *she* say? Who was this person who was suddenly turning her life upside down?

Then Courtney collected her thoughts. A copy of the university directory was in her room. All she had to do was look up the number and pick up the phone.

"Diane," Courtney said suddenly. "Look, sorry I'm out of it. There's something I have to do now, but let's walk over to the party together in about an hour."

"I'll knock on your door," Diane called out as Courtney slipped quickly up the staircase. In a moment, she was alone in her room, staring at her telephone with an agonizing mixture of terror and longing. All she had to do was pick up the phone. In a moment, perhaps, she could have him on the line.

Courtney rapidly flipped through the student directory until she found his off-campus apartment phone number. Then taking a deep breath, she dialed the number and waited desperately for Dash's phone to ring. For once in her life, Coutney had no idea what she would say.

"Hi," Dash's taped yet still sexy voice blared

from an answering machine. The sound of shuffling papers and distant jazz could be heard. *"Uh, this is Dash Ramirez. I'm not here. Leave a message after the beep. Oh, yeah, and if this is Steve Christensen, your story is due eight A.M. Sunday, man. No excuses. And you owe me five bucks. BEEEEEEEEEEEEP."*

Still holding the phone, Courtney laid back on her bed. It was easy for her to relax now that she only had to talk to a machine. She could take her time. Wing it.

"Hi, Dash," Courtney began slowly, stunned by the sultry tone in her voice. "Um, I just wanted to follow up on our conversation the other day—about the rummage sale? You were right. The idea is dull and we really do need help with promotion. Well, maybe not the really silly stuff you were suggesting. But I think you were on the right track." Courtney paused, wondering if she were talking too long. Was the machine still on? "Why don't you stop by tomorrow—Sunday—at noon? We can talk then. Okay? Bye."

Courtney slowly set the phone back on the hook and stared up at her bedroom ceiling. She hadn't felt this way since she was twelve and in love with the boy who sat behind her in math.

Her heart was racing like a madwoman and her hands were like ice. She had done it. She had actually picked up the phone and done the impossible. She'd been wild. Reckless.

And she had no idea what would happen next.

Ten

....

Winnie stood precariously on a table full of red hotline phones, scanning the crush of Health Fair goers for Josh and her banners. By eleven o'clock, the fair was jammed and the noise was deafening. Winnie's desperation was growing by the second.

"Winnie!" Teresa Grey, the hotline's codirector, ran up, ducking between a roasted peanut cart and a nurse offering on-the-spot blood pressure tests. "Where are those banners? We're lost without them. No one knows who we are!"

"Josh will be here any minute," Winnie yelled

over the pounding music, struggling to hold back the panic in her voice. "You are going to absolutely love them." She climbed down from the table and looked back at the display. Without her beautiful banners, the hotline booth was a boring, disastrous gray skeleton of an exhibit.

The Crisis Hotline people had been depending on her. If Josh didn't show up with the banners, they'd probably ditch her as a volunteer. No more counseling. No more on-the-job crisis training. One of the best parts of her life would be up in smoke.

Except for the banners, everything was in place. The phone lines had been transferred temporarily to the floor of the gym and three volunteers were already working on a number of morning-after distress calls. They had books on coping with stress, brochures on anger, pamphlets on grief. In an hour, the drama department would be arriving to stage an impromptu "fair fighting" demonstration.

But with no banners, all they looked like was a bunch of people selling insurance over the phone.

Winnie nervously played with the starfish on her neon fishnet purse.

I'm not going to explode. When I see Josh I'm going to be calm. Josh and I love each other and we are not going to run away from problems. I'm ready for this, aren't I? I'm a trained counselor in fair fighting. I know how to show my anger in constructive ways.

Winnie looked around at the exasperated stares she was getting from the other hotline workers. She suddenly wished she hadn't worn her glow-in-the-dark orange Lycra bodysuit over her black-and-orange, tiger-striped T-shirt. Right now, she wanted to shrink into the background.

She shut her eyes and said a small prayer. Josh *had* seen her scribbled note reminding him about the banners. He *had* bought the station wagon. He *was* on his way. She could depend on him, just like she always had—and always would.

Winnie bit hard on the side of her lip. Any minute, she would see him coming toward her in the crowd. He'd smile his gentle smile and kiss her lightly on the lips. They'd tell each other how sorry they were for fighting last night. Together, they'd agree that when two incredibly dynamic people get married, there were bound to be mixups—pressures.

A lump was growing in her throat. Winnie

hadn't actually talked with Josh since their fight the night before. He'd stumbled in way after she'd returned from her late shift at the hotline.

When she awoke that morning, his warm back was curled next to her stomach and there was a peaceful, little-boy look on his smooth face. It almost made her forget their fight and she had been tempted to wake him and ask him if he'd seen the beautiful apartment. Instead, she'd decided to let him rest.

"We need those banners," Teresa said out loud. "If people don't know we're here, people won't use the service. And if no one uses it, our funding will dry up in a flash!"

Winnie nodded, watching a group of students pass the booth with questioning looks.

"Is this the fair information booth?" one girl asked. "We're looking for the rest rooms."

"The rest rooms?" Winnie heard Teresa shriek. "We spend all that money to transfer the phones and arrange for a booth—and—and people are asking us directions for rest rooms!?"

"Come on, Teresa," called out one of the hotline volunteers. "Get a grip. The banners will be here, just like Winnie promised."

Winnie sank helplessly down on a folding chair and stared at her glossy sunset-orange nails, her eyes slowly filling with tears. Josh wouldn't let her down at a time like this. *Would he?*

She glanced at her watch again. Maybe something had happened to Josh. Had Mikoto's station wagon turned out to be a dangerous heap of junk with no brakes? Had it caught on fire? Maybe Josh was lying somewhere with his poor head crushed and bleeding into the windshield of the car.

"Teresa!" Winnie jumped up, her Wilma Flintstone earrings banging against the side of her face. "I have to find Josh."

"I agree. Just find him fast," Teresa said, cupping her hand over a hotline call she'd just answered.

Winnie hooked on her belt pack and ran out of the noisy gymnasium into the soft spring morning. Tearing through the gym parking lot, Winnie desperately searched for Mikoto's station wagon. Not catching sight of it, she decided to run through the lots surrounding the adjacent life sciences building, then head off campus to check the apartment.

It was now eleven-thirty—two and a half hours after Josh was supposed to have arrived. Her heart pumping with worry, Winnie took a shortcut behind the pancake house and ducked into a back alley littered with overturned garbage cans, finally emerging onto grimy Neptune Avenue.

When she reached Lauren's former apartment house, she shoved open the front door and stepped inside.

Her mouth dropped open. The lobby looked as if it had been vandalized by some of the hoods who hung around the pawnshop at the end of the block.

Then, slowly, she began to realize that the stuff heaped all over the filthy floor was— *HERS!*

Winnie gasped out loud at the mess. Smashed at the bottom of the stairs were her precious Hawaiian paper lanterns covered with hula dancers. A cardboard box containing all of her high-school memorabilia, along with an assortment of poodle skirts, baseball hats, and Supergirl comic books lay squashed in the middle of the floor, as if someone had thrown it down three flights of stairs. Poster tubes, dirty clothes, and the contents of their refrigerator were everywhere.

Not believing her eyes, Winnie waded through the strewn articles, picking some up and putting them aside. Then she flung off a sleeping bag that was draped over something huge near the stair railings. Her heart stopped. A massive motorcycle was underneath, gleaming in the dimly lit lobby. Winnie recognized the motorcycle as Peter Dvorsky's, but she couldn't fathom what it was doing there.

Faint sounds from above made her look up. She saw Josh emerge at the top of the first flight of stairs. He was moving backward slowly, dragging a large plastic garbage bag.

"Josh!" Winnie cried out. "What happened?"

She watched him straighten up and look at her with a stony face. "It's moving day, Winnie," he snapped. "Remember?"

"But, Josh, I thought we agreed that you would bring my banners to the Health Fair. I came back here because you didn't show."

Josh said not a word. Instead, he bent down to stuff junk that had scattered on the landing into the bag.

Winnie sighed. As a volunteer at the Crisis Hotline, she knew staying calm was the only way to get results. "Why don't you let me have the keys to the station wagon," she said sensibly. "I'll drive the banners over myself."

"I can't, Winnie. I didn't buy the station wagon," Josh said, looking down at her and wiping his hands on the front of his torn sweat-shirt. His pants were grimy, his eyes were bloodshot, and he looked like he hadn't shaved in two days. "I bought Peter's motorcycle instead."

Winnie stood glued to the spot. Her lips began to quiver. "You what?"

"I bought Peter's bike."

Anger and indignation were beginning to snake through Winnie's body. "You—you bought a motorcycle?" she whispered. "But I'm terrified of them."

"You are?" Josh twisted the top of the garbage bag and pulled a tie out of his back pocket. "You never told me that."

"A friend of mine from high school had a real bad accident on a bike. I was riding with him. I was just bruised, but he ended up with a rup-tured spleen and spent months in the hospital. He could have died," Winnie said. She began to cry. "Couldn't you have asked me what I thought first? We're married now. We're sup-posed to consult each other before making big decisions. And we'd agreed to buy a car!"

Josh dropped the garbage bag and looked at her. His face looked suddenly pale and drained. "So now you're feeling practical. *Now* you want to go the safe route?" he shouted. "Well, just because *you're* the one who's in a jam this time doesn't mean you can get your way. The other day you wanted to spend my parents' money on *a hotel suite*!"

"Keep it down out there," Mrs. Calvin yelled as she jerked open her door. "If you kids don't shut up and have all your stuff cleared out of here in an hour, I'll call the police!"

Josh ignored the landlady. He descended the stairs two at a time and his voice continued to rise with each step. "Did you ask *me* first before you dumped six hundred and fifty dollars on that shoe box of an apartment that doesn't even have a decent plug for a hot plate—much less for a computer?" he shouted

Winnie stood there, speechless, as Josh approached her. He was really angry. She'd never seen him like this.

"Did you ask *me* before you ran off to the fair," Josh went on. "Don't tell me you forgot this was moving day?"

Tears were pouring down Winnie's cheeks. "Josh," she said softly. "Please!"

"Did you ask me before you decided to paint banners all week instead of packing your vast collection of junk? The new tenant is here, Winnie, just like Mrs. Calvin told us he would be. I couldn't move everything fast enough for her, so she personally threw your stuff down the stairwell to make room for him." He was standing right in front of her now, and he pointed at all that lay scattered about them. "Maybe you'd at least like to tell me what I should do with all of this?!"

Suddenly, Winnie saw red. Her whole body exploding with fury and sadness and frustration, she grabbed the plastic garbage bag from him and ripped off the tie.

"This is what you can do with it, Josh Gaffey," Winnie yelled, dumping the bag upside down. A small hill of old Christmas cards, party hats, record album covers, and cheap paperbacks formed at his feet.

"And *this* . . ." Winnie picked up a broken blow dryer and threw it at Josh, narrowly missing his astonished head. Next she grabbed a box of grape Jell-O and sent it flying into his knee. "And this here!" she yelled, flinging an orange ankle boot into a dead potted plant. "I don't care what you do with this stuff. I don't care about *any* of it anymore. You can throw it all away. You can throw *me* away."

Tears streaming down her face, Winnie continued to hurl things at Josh as he slowly backed up toward his motorcycle. Everything was lost. Down the drain. She'd been wrong about him.

"You can take these, too, and throw them away," Winnie sobbed, throwing her Rollerblades against the wall. *"You can throw our marriage away!"*

Josh's jaw clenched shut and he simply jerked the motorcycle around and started rolling it out the front door.

"Or you can stick our marriage vows on that deathmobile and crash the whole crazy idea into a brick wall!" Winnie cried.

She collapsed at the bottom of the stairs as she heard Josh rev up the engine and roar off.

"We'll never make this work," Winnie murmured, staring numbly at the battlefield before her feet. "It's too hard. It's just too hard."

Eleven

Lauren looked up absently from a thick book of modern dance photographs and surveyed Kimberly's dorm room. Leotards, lab books, and sheets of opera scores belonging to Kimberly's roommate, Freya, were scattered haphazardly about. Kimberly was sprawled on the floor and Faith was tenderly feeding Oreo cookies to a distraught Winnie, who was buried beneath a quilt.

"What time is it?" Lauren asked tiredly. It was good to be with her friends, but she knew she'd soon have to face Melissa. And she was dreading it.

"Seven," Kimberly said, glumly dipping a tortilla chip into a plastic container of bean dip on the floor. She looked over at Winnie and Faith. "How's Winnie doing?"

Faith shrugged and stuffed her hand into the half-empty package. "Want another, Win?"

Lauren watched Winnie's hand emerge from under the quilt and take the cookie. The quilt began to shudder and she could hear Winnie begin to sob.

A few hours ago, Lauren had stopped by to see if Kimberly had recovered from her panic attack earlier in the day at the Health Fair. But shortly after she arrived, they heard Winnie pounding desperately on Faith's door. Faith immediately whisked an hysterical Winnie next door to Kimberly's room—away from Faith's sharp-tongued roommate, Liza Ruff.

Now, all Lauren could see were the tips of Winnie's spiky hair sticking out from underneath Kimberly's blanket. Surrounding the bed were piles of wadded-up pink tissues. From what Lauren could gather, Winnie had been badly shaken by a fight she'd had with Josh that morning.

"Men are thoughtless, unreliable, spoiled, selfish, idiotic beasts," Kimberly said, tiredly rolling over on her back. She grabbed the bag of chips and placed them on top of her loose workout shirt. "What is it with men? They seem to think we're so desperate for them—that we'll do anything!"

Faith looked over at Lauren and rolled her eyes. Winnie's blanket began shaking as she let out another long sob.

Lauren felt terrible for Winnie. Just yesterday Winnie had been so deliriously happy when they found the little Victorian apartment. It seemed incredible that in a few short hours, her friend could collapse into a heap of utter despair.

Yesterday, Lauren would have completely agreed with Kimberly about men.

But today was different. She'd seen Dash.

"Kimberly, you're not helping things," Faith said quietly.

"But it's true," Kimberly said, staring dejectedly at the ceiling. "Winnie needs to know that she's not alone. The trouble with men is that they are completely self-centered! Look at Derek. Flaky and unreliable. And Clifford Bronton. Who did he think he was, giving me that big buildup?"

Faith gave Kimberly an exasperated look. Her blond hair was pulled back in a French braid and she looked exhausted from trying to cheer Winnie up.

"Kimberly, you don't really know Clifford. He might be really nice. And you probably hurt his feelings."

"Are you kidding?" Kimberly said defensively, lifting herself up into a sitting position. "I know Clifford, and he is definitely not the type to get all worked up about. He's a totally serious, egghead science nerd. He will definitely survive."

"Right," Faith replied sarcastically. "He's a great student, so he probably has no heart." She teasingly shook her finger at Kimberly. "He sends beautiful messages and lovely bunches of flowers, so he's probably really insensitive."

Kimberly sullenly stabbed the bean dip with a broken chip.

"And Josh is not self-centered, flaky, and unreliable," Lauren spoke up.

"*MMNNNUUHHMMMMMNNNUH,*" Winnie bellowed something from under her blanket.

Lauren looked in Winnie's direction. Something made her want to shake some sense into Winnie's mixed-up head. It was clear that Josh was a great guy and they were meant for each other. "Give him a chance," she heard herself say. "Maybe he's just as confused and upset as you are. You two have been through a lot in the past week."

Winnie suddenly shot up in the bed and fixed her eyes on Lauren. Lauren's mouth half dropped open when she saw Winnie's ragged face. Mascara was running down her white cheeks, her lips were purply, and her clumpy hair was smashed up against one side of her head.

"Did you give Dash another chance after he humiliated *you*?" Winnie burst out. "After he tried to take all the credit for your journalism award and then slammed the door in your face when you got even?"

Lauren felt as if Winnie had shot an arrow through her heart. She stared back at her, overcome with surprise and recognition.

"No, I didn't give him another chance, Winnie. And now I wish I had," she heard herself say. "People don't always agree. People don't always listen to one another. Being in love doesn't change all that. But if you really love someone, you go back. You try again."

Winnie shook her head. "That's easy to say," she sobbed, yanking another tissue out of the box and blowing her nose loudly. "But I don't think Josh really cared about the work I put into those banners. What matters to him are his computer programs." Winnie stabbed an index finger into the air. "Computer programs: number one." Two fingers went up. "Winnie Gottlieb: number two. And it will never be any different."

"Come on, Win." Faith rubbed Winnie's back. "Take a deep breath. You two need some time to straighten your thoughts out, that's all."

"No way," Winnie declared, clutching the edge of Kimberly's bed with her orange nails and staring down as if she were about to jump off a cliff. "This is it. My life is over. Only eighteen years old, and I've managed to ruin a perfectly good life."

"Winnie," Faith exclaimed.

"My marriage is over."

"You don't mean that," Lauren said, impulsively standing up and walking over to the window.

"It was a terrible idea," Winnie said simply. "I don't know why I thought it would work. Divorced. Eighteen and divorced after one week. No. Eighteen and widowed."

"Widowed?" Kimberly turned around slowly and looked at Winnie.

"Yeah!" Winnie said, her wild eyes blazing.

"He's probably dead right now, from a motorcycle accident. Tomorrow's obit will start: Thrown into an oncoming Mack truck as the deathmobile skids around the curve . . ."

"The what?" Lauren stammered.

There was a sudden knock on Kimberly's door and all four heads turned.

"Oh my god!" Winnie whispered. "Please let it be Josh!"

Lauren walked over and opened the door. A short, pleasant-faced guy wearing a conservative button-down shirt stood in the hall. His hands were casually slipped into his blue jeans and he had a friendly, straightforward smile that Lauren liked immediately.

"Hi. Is Kimberly in?" the guy asked. "Tell her Clifford Bronton is here to see her."

Lauren opened the door wider and looked back helplessly at Kimberly, who remained passively on the floor, her eyes growing bigger by the second.

"Oh, there she is." Clifford stepped in politely. "Hi, Kimberly."

Kimberly gave him a guilty look. "Hi, Clifford."

"Look, Kimberly," Clifford began matter-of-factly, "I know that you saw me at the Health Fair, wearing the hat."

"I—I," Kimberly stammered.

"Come on," Clifford interrupted. "You saw me. You didn't like what you saw. And you left. Simple as that."

"Clifford . . ." Lauren watched Kimberly struggle pitifully for words, reminded painfully of her own awkward encounter with Dash that morning.

"You didn't even bother to hear me out," Clifford continued calmly. "And you knew how I felt about you."

"Clifford . . ." Kimberly stood up slowly and walked toward him. Lauren saw that Kimberly towered over him, and that Clifford didn't care.

"Is it that easy for you to walk away?" Clifford asked, tilting his head back a little as she drew closer. "Do you throw people away that easily?"

Kimberly instinctively drew a hand up to her mouth. "No, Clifford. No . . ."

"Look, if you're really that thoughtless and shallow, then I'm sorry I ever bothered you," he said, shrugging and slipping his hands into his blue jeans. "I won't do it again, you can be sure. It's just that something tells me you're not. Maybe you were scared. Maybe you got stage fright. You told me once that's why you quit dancing."

"Yes," Kimberly said softly, not taking her eyes off him.

"If you have any character at all, meet me for coffee in the student union at nine o'clock tomorrow morning," Clifford said, moving toward the door. "Hear me out, Kimberly."

Lauren took a deep breath as Clifford closed the door, marveling at the proud, straightforward way he'd confronted Kimberly. Couldn't Kimberly see what a lump she'd been? Wasn't she totally embarrassed at herself for not giving him a chance? Lauren sat slowly back down on Kimberly's bed. Was she thinking about Kimberly—or herself?

"*That* was the absolutely *terrible* guy you've been avoiding all day?" Faith asked incredulously. "Are you crazy, Kimberly? The guy is fantastic. A gem."

Winnie pulled out a tissue and began wiping the mascara off her face. "He's got guts, character, and class." She shrugged. "So what if he's a little short? He's cuddly."

After a few moments, a dazed Kimberly left to take a hot shower. And while Faith and Winnie began to talk quietly about high school guys, Lauren suddenly remembered the clipping that Dash had handed her at the Health Fair.

Carefully, she pulled it from her purse, unfolded it, and smoothed it out on her lap. When she looked at the headline, her heart stopped. It was a boxed column with Dash's byline on it. *"Breaking Up Is Hard To Do"—Why Does the Girl Always Get To Sing That Song? By Dash Ramirez.*

Lauren sat up and pushed her glasses up on her nose. As she read, her eyes began to fill slowly with tears.

Okay. Okay. Dash's column began on a humorous note. *I broke up with my girlfriend recently. Let's get that out of the way. It happened to me. Not my roommate. Not my brother or the guy at the hardware store. I usually get to write about other people's problems. But not today. This story is about me.*

Lauren's throat swelled with longing and pride as she continued reading his piece. It was as if he'd written a letter to her—in the only way he knew how.

Why is it that women get all the sympathy and kindness when they break up with someone they love? When a guy is suddenly cut loose, he gets nothing but slaps of congratulations and exaggerated winks. His friends try to fix him up. Women approach him with a boldness unheard of in his high school days.

Everyone's waiting for him to make a move, not realizing that he's lost at sea, vulnerable to the slightest swell, the merest puff of wind. Anything and everything sends him off course . . .

Lauren let the clipping slip down to her knees, tears spilling down her round cheeks. Dash was reaching out to her. And now it was up to her. What was she waiting for? It was time she read her own heart.

Do you throw people away that easily? Clifford's question hung in her brain like a light bulb that he'd just turned on. She missed Dash—desperately. She loved him. And she was finally ready to do something about it.

There was another knock at the door and the three of them looked up, wondering what crazy thing was going to happen next. Their faces fell, however, when they saw KC's ashen face peer into the room. She looked terrified.

"KC!" Faith cried out, springing up. "What's happened?"

KC stepped into the room, her dark hair hanging in strings and her gray eyes wild with fright. Lauren knew something had to be terribly wrong when she saw that KC had thrown on a wrinkled tweed blazer that clashed horribly with her spring shirtwaist dress.

"I—uh—I," KC began, muttering in confusion.

"What is it?" Faith took her shoulders in alarm. "Is it your dad?"

KC's head was nodding wordlessly and her mouth began to quiver. She sat down and placed her trembling hand on her forehead. "I—I ran over here," she choked the words out. "Mom called. Dad's in Jacksonville Memorial. His—uh—shortness of breath got really bad, so they had to put him on oxygen around the clock. I guess it's really put a strain on his heart. She—they—want me to come home."

"Oh, KC," Faith hugged her, unable to hold back her own tears. "What can we do to help?"

As Lauren looked on numbly, Winnie stood up and moved toward KC. Lauren could practically see a visible change in Winnie, as if she were mentally throwing out her own problems to make room for her friend's.

Winnie slipped her hand against KC's shaking back. "This isn't happening," Winnie murmured. "Not to him. Not to your dad."

Wiping the tears rolling down her face, KC pulled back and tried to talk. "I called the bus station. And—and the bus. The bus. It doesn't leave until tomorrow afternoon."

"What?" Faith whispered.

KC began to sound as if she were totally disoriented. "The bus," KC repeated. "The rummage sale. The Tri Betas . . . I, uh . . ."

"KC," Faith said firmly. "Forget the rummage sale. We're going to get you home. You don't have to worry about anything. We'll take care of it."

"Take my Jeep," Lauren said, taking the key to the Jeep off her chain and handing it to Faith. "I'll stay here and let Courtney know what's happened. She'll understand."

KC looked at her, as if she were trying hard to focus. "Thanks."

"Come on, KC," Winnie murmured. "We're with you. We're going to take care of everything and get you home."

Faith narrowed her eyes. "Winnie? Are you okay? Are you sure you can go?"

"I'm absolutely sure," Winnie said, pulling on her jingle-bell boots. "The rest of this stuff with Josh will just have to wait."

Faith dug through her purse. "Do you have cash?"

"I've got ten dollars," Winnie said hurriedly, hooking her fishnet bag over her shoulder and taking KC's other arm. "What's the gas tank like, Lauren?"

"Full."

"Okay." Faith pulled open the door. "Let's fly. If we leave now, we'll be in Jacksonville before ten."

"Drive carefully," Lauren murmured to herself as she stood helplessly in the middle of Kimberly's room, watching the three loyal friends disappear into the hall.

The dorm room was quiet, as if a wild storm had blown through, leaving Lauren breathless, her heart stripped of all feeling except one— love.

Winnie, Faith, and KC had shown her what love in a friendship was all about. There was nothing more important.

Slowly, calmly, Lauren stood up and looked out the window. All of a sudden she knew what she had to do. She'd sleep now. And tomorrow afternoon, she'd call Dash.

Love and friendship.

He was the one person who was offering her both.

Twelve

Kimberly's alarm was screaming.

She reached her long arm up, grabbed the clock off a stack of physics workbooks, and stuffed it under her pillow.

Curling back up in her comfy flannel sheets, Kimberly closed her eyes and thought about last night. When she'd returned from her shower, Winnie and Faith had just left and Lauren was waiting to tell her the bad news about Mr. Angeletti.

Kimberly turned over on her side. Propped up next to her bed was a framed photograph taken of her and her mother ecstatically hugging at an opening night gala in San Antonio. Both were wearing Billie Holiday-style gardenias in their hair and identical grins on their faces. They almost looked like sisters.

Kimberly sighed. Like KC and her dad, Kimberly and her mother had their differences. But she couldn't imagine how horrible it would be if her mother were suddenly sick.

She swallowed hard and looked over at Freya, sleeping peacefully under a huge Pavarotti poster on the wall. Just thinking about KC's life-and-death problems made her own problems seem petty. Why was she making such a fuss over Clifford, anyway? Faith was right. She probably *had* hurt him. Why was she trying to turn him into such a monster?

Kimberly sat up, suddenly remembering why she'd set the alarm.

Clifford.

Nine o'clock sharp, Sunday morning.

Student union snack bar.

If she had any character at all . . .

Kimberly shot up in bed, found the alarm clock, and held it in front of her bleary eyes. Eight fifty-five, the digital readout blinked.

"Oh, no," she muttered, dragging herself up and

sleepily pulling on a pair of leggings and a baggy gray sweatshirt hanging from her study lamp. Her face stared dully back at her in the mirror.

"I can't do this," she whispered. She frowned and slipped her hair into a ponytail. "Yes I can. I have to do this. He's a human being. He's my friend."

Kimberly continued to urge herself on as she let herself out the door and into the quiet, empty hall. A door opened and a girl with disheveled hair and baggy socks wandered sleepily toward the women's bathroom.

Kimberly slowly let herself down the stairway. The only sign of life in the dorm was a distant string quartet recording and two dance majors limbering up in the lobby.

"People are crazy to meet so early on a Sunday," Kimberly began grumbling quietly to herself. "It's ungodly."

She was still muttering under her breath as her long legs carried her impatiently into the student union snack bar. She glanced sleepily about the empty room and was just about to leave when she saw Clifford sitting by himself at a corner table.

"Kimberly!" He half stood up and raised his hand.

Kimberly stopped, dazed, and stared at his friendly, alert smile. She walked slowly toward him. Clearly, Clifford had been at the table for a while. A Sunday paper was spread out in front of him. It looked like he'd almost finished a cup of coffee and a piece of toast.

"I got here a little early," Clifford explained, folding up part of the paper to make room for her. "It was such a beautiful morning, I went on a bike ride east of town to see the sun come up."

Kimberly stared at him, then rubbed her scratchy eyes. "You did?"

"Would you like some coffee?" Clifford asked casually, as if he were used to meeting people so early in the morning.

"Yes. Please."

Kimberly watched him walk to the counter, pour a cup, and pay for it. She was having a little difficulty imagining Clifford riding a bike all that way. But then, maybe he wasn't really pudgy. He was just short. In fact, he could be a solid hunk of muscle under his preppie clothes, for all she knew. This morning, he wore a navy-blue hooded sweatshirt and jeans. Still hooked to his ankles were his aluminum bicycling clips. A neon belt pack lay at his feet.

Clifford set the cup of coffee down in front of her and settled back into his seat, tucking his hands comfortably inside the front pocket of his sweatshirt. He looked at her sympathetically through his glasses. "Wake up, Kimberly. If not for me, for your grade point average. You've got a Maxfield lab quiz coming up tomorrow."

"Yeah, right."

"Look, Kimberly," Clifford began. "I know I was kind of hard on you last night. I shouldn't have blasted you like that in front of your friends. I'm sorry."

Kimberly shrugged and looked down. She wasn't prepared to say anything yet. At least until she had a few more sips of coffee.

"In fact," Clifford went on, looking sheepish, "the whole business of secret flowers and notes—was—was kind of dumb, I guess. I should have come right out and told you. I had no right to get you all worked up. It was just that . . ."

"What?" Kimberly looked up at Clifford's embarrassed face. "It was just that—what?"

Clifford studied his coffee cup. "I just didn't want to come right out and say it."

"Why not?" Kimberly asked.

"Because I knew you'd say no," Clifford said

simply, looking at her straight in the eye. "I thought I'd have a chance if you really knew how I felt first. But then, I was wrong, wasn't I?"

Kimberly felt herself soften inside. "Clifford, I . . ."

"I know I'm not the hunk you always hoped to meet." Here he was, at the crack of dawn, baring his soul to her with so much grace, honesty, and self-deprecating humor that Kimberly was taken aback. "You've told me enough about Derek Weldon. I know the kind of guy you're attracted to."

Kimberly's mouth was beginning to fall open. Clifford didn't mince words.

"Big and tall and black and beautiful," Clifford continued, a warm, understanding smile sneaking out of the corner of his lips. "Right? Well, look what tall and beautiful got you."

"Disappointment," Kimberly whispered, her eyes drifting out of the window to the dewy lawn, where a couple of guys in shorts had already started throwing a Frisbee.

"Kimberly," Clifford said, leaning forward earnestly. "You haven't given me a chance. Look, I know you. And I like who you *are*. We have fun together in lab. We talk. We joke. I've never met anyone like you. You're brainy, witty, gutsy . . ." He held his palms up in exasperation. "I'd almost prefer it if you were a clumsy, overweight wall flower with thick glasses. Then there wouldn't be so many obstacles."

Kimberly smiled. She was beginning to feel warm and relaxed, as if she were talking with a best friend—not a guy who was trying to come on to her. Derek had been exciting, but he'd also made her feel anxious and angry most of the time. Clifford was right. They *did* have fun together. And what was more important? Having a great time together with someone, or having some arrogant, handsome hunk to drool all over?

"Looks aren't everything," Clifford said teasingly, as if he sensed a turning tide. "Give me a chance. I've got a lot to offer. Look. Give me one evening. One date. We'll have some dinner somewhere, then maybe see a movie. Or maybe we'll just talk. Whatever feels right to you."

"Okay." Kimberly grinned, bending forward over her cup, and looking Clifford right in the eye. "Okay, Doctor Bronton. Pick me up at seven o'clock tonight."

Clifford flopped back in his seat and allowed a huge smile to spread across his face. He tilted his head a little. "Just like that? We've got a date?"

"Just like that," Kimberly answered, wondering why she had been such a shallow, impatient jerk with Clifford. She hadn't met a guy this honest and determined in her life. "There's just one thing."

"Say it. It's yours," Clifford replied, happily balling up a napkin and tossing it at her.

"How about another cup of coffee?"

It was early Sunday afternoon, and Courtney was finally alone on the stone terrace in back of the Tri Beta house. Stretched on a cushiony lounge chair, she flipped open her leather organizer and began surveying her checklist of rummage sale donations.

She squinted up into the warm sun. Why couldn't she concentrate?

Dash Ramirez. Dash Ramirez. Dash Ramirez.

Her brain had been whirring with his name all morning as she picked through boxes of junk and directed truckloads of furniture into the sorority's elegant mansion. Had yesterday been a dream? Or had she actually picked up the phone and invited Dash to help her promote the rummage sale?

Dash was cocky, tough, and looked like he

didn't have a dime to his name. She was well mannered, well brought up, and was used to moving in wealthy, educated circles. A wave of unfamiliar panic suddenly rippled through her. What had she been thinking of? Even if he did show up at her prim sorority house, he'd probably laugh in her face. Then what would she do? Slip back into her dreamlike role of Tri Beta President Courtney Conner? Efficient, organized, predictable, unchanging Courtney Conner?

She stared down at the mundane figures in her organizer, wondering if her life would always be this way. Was it supposed to be? Or was her chance encounter with Dash at the bookstore last week a signal that there was something more?

What would she be willing to risk in order to find out?

"Courtney!" Annette stuck her head out of the French doors. "Look at this darling antique bird cage old Mrs. Hollingsworth donated."

"Wonderful!" Courtney called out, even though she knew Annette was just trying to stroke her by putting the brightest face on the whole disastrous fund-raising event.

As expected, the donations were as dull as the

inside of a thrift store warehouse. The house was now filled with old typewriters, worn clothing, mismatched chairs, and beat-up bicycles. The event wasn't likely to bring in more than five hundred dollars, while Diane's glittering auction idea could have made a few thousand.

"Hi, Courtney," she heard a quiet voice above her. Courtney looked up from her figures and almost stopped breathing when she saw that it was Lauren.

Wearing steel-rimmed glasses, an old work shirt, and a pair of white painter's dungarees, Lauren looked like her usual distracted, creative self. Even though Lauren had dropped the Tri Betas, Courtney had always admired her quiet intelligence and her courageous work at the *Journal*. Still, she didn't exactly look like the slim, exotic type she imagined Dash would be attracted to. It was strange to think that Lauren and Dash were once together.

"Lauren, how nice to see you," Courtney greeted her. She sat up and put her book down. Trying to act calm, she curled up her legs and patted the lounge chair. "Have a seat."

"It's about KC," Lauren said. "I have a message from her." She turned her sad, violet eyes toward Courtney and twisted the leather strap on her beaded purse. "Her dad is getting worse. She had to go home. I'm not sure about this, but I think he may be dying."

"Oh, no," Courtney whispered, covering her mouth. "Poor KC."

"She went back to Jacksonville last night with Faith and Winnie," Lauren explained. "She wanted you to know that's why she wasn't here today helping with the rummage sale."

"Her father is in the hospital and she's thinking about the rummage sale?" Courtney murmured, staring out at the tall trees surrounding the Tri Beta house. She stood up and paced back and forth on the flagstone patio. "I wonder if I should page her at the hospital? Show her a little support, you know. Or maybe I should jump in the car now and drive out to Jacksonville."

"Why don't you give it a little time?" Lauren suggested. "She's probably pretty distracted now."

Courtney nodded, suddenly remembering Dash and the silly phone call, which now seemed like an embarrassing, childish mistake. And he could show up at any minute.

"Thanks for letting me know about this, Lauren." Courtney gave her an anxious glance.

"Why don't you go inside and have something cool to drink? I'm sure a few of your old sisters would like to say hello."

"Okay." Lauren shrugged. "I'll check out the rummage sale stuff, too. Never know what you'll find."

Courtney slipped a pair of sunglasses on as Lauren wandered inside. She still had another half an hour on rummage sale duty, so spotting a few straggling dandelions sprouting in the patio's flower boxes, Courtney knelt down and began furiously weeding. Her thoughts were so confused by the news about KC that she almost hoped Dash wouldn't show.

Then Courtney heard the back gate open and close—and the sound of approaching footsteps.

"Uh, hi," she heard a voice behind her.

Courtney turned slowly around and saw Dash. Wearing a faded black T-shirt and a pair of torn jeans, Dash looked like his usual, sloppy self. But something was different about him today. He actually looked a little uncomfortable.

"Hello, Dash," Courtney tried to say casually as he walked slowly over to the patio. "I'm glad you came."

"Uh, yeah," Dash said. He stopped, coughed, and looked away. "Sure."

Courtney watched speechlessly as Dash sat down on the edge of an elegant wrought-iron garden chair. His right ankle was nervously bumping up and down on his knee and he was looking intently away from her, almost as if he wished he were someplace else.

"Well, uh—thanks for stopping by," Courtney finally said, trying desperately to think of what to do next. She wasn't used to feeling this unsure of herself. Her heart was sputtering inside of her like a schoolgirl on her first date. "Um, before we start, let me get a piece of paper and pencil. I want to write your ideas down."

Dash's dark eyes looked momentarily confused. "I didn't think I—I *could* come, but—uh—someone canceled an editorial meeting on me, so I had some free time."

"Oh."

"Yeah." Dash's glance moved away, then returned and held hers. He shrugged. "So, I'm here. At your service. Just tell me what you need to know."

"Well." Courtney racked her brain for something to ask. "Do you think we should advertise in the *Journal*?" She winced. This was incredibly dumb. Dash was going to see right through her.

Dash settled back into the chair and smiled at her. "Sure. And I'll give you a good rate."

Courtney gave a short laugh.

"Hey, you know more about promotion than this, Courtney." Dash gave her a questioning look. "You probably know more than I do."

There was a long silence as Courtney pretended to write something down.

Dash stirred uncomfortably in his seat. "Look, if you asked me over because you wanted to talk about something else, that's okay. Let's just cut to the real topic. Is something going on with the Greeks? Do you have some information the *Journal* could use?"

Courtney was so nervous she could barely sit still. His black eyes were flashing at her. Her mouth dropped open to say something, but nothing came out. She wasn't going to be able to keep this act up for long.

"Something *is* going on," Dash said, straightening up. His eyes darted up toward the house. "What is it?"

"No," Courtney said abruptly.

"No what?" Dash persisted. His eyes roamed the landscaped backyard as if he wanted to remember every detail. "You changed your mind? You're not going to tell me?"

Courtney shuddered. She was finding it difficult to breathe, even in the fresh air and the blinding sunshine. Unable to stay in her seat any longer, she suddenly stood up and ran her hand through her hair.

"Look, Dash," Courtney began nervously. "I'm sorry I called you. I just . . ."

"What?" Dash stood up and walked toward her. Courtney hadn't realized how tall he was. He was clean-shaven for once, and she detected a faint, lemony scent as he drew closer. "Tell me."

"I—I just wanted to see you again, Dash," Courtney finally said. "I'm sorry."

"Sorry?" Dash held his ground, looking curiously into her eyes. He gave a half laugh. "It's okay. These days when anyone calls me, I just do what they say."

"You do?" Courtney whispered, stepping even closer, barely aware of what she was doing. It was as if a strange and magical curtain had settled down around them and everything else in the world had disappeared. She forgot everything. The Tri Betas. The rummage sale. Her classes. Her meetings. She forgot Courtney Conner.

All she could see was the dark, curious face in

front of hers. She felt her right hand rise up and slip about his bare, tawny neck.

Dash's eyes opened wide. "Courtney? What are you . . ."

"I don't know. I don't know," Courtney murmured, unable to believe what she was doing. In a moment, she'd found his lips and was pressing them gently to hers. To her utter amazement, Dash began to kiss her back. His lips were warm and he smelled faintly of leather and lemony after-shave. His strong arm was pressing into her back, pulling her toward him. She felt dizzy and knew she'd fall back into the lounge chair if Dash let go of her.

She looked up and steadied herself. Was he playing with her? Her heart was thudding in her throat and she once again had that terrifying feeling of not knowing what would happen next. Her life was suddenly and totally out of control.

Then, slowly, she noticed a figure moving in the background over Dash's shoulder. The French doors leading to the back terrace had opened, and someone stepped out. Courtney looked up.

It was Lauren.

In a split second, Courtney saw Lauren look at them, first with amusement, then with horror, when she realized that the guy was Dash. Her hand reached up to her startled mouth, and in an instant, Lauren had fled back through the doors and into the house.

Unaware of what was going on behind him, Dash loosened his hold on Courtney and stepped back a little, looking completely stunned. They stood there in the bright sun, staring at each other.

And for the first time, neither one of them knew what to say.

Thirteen

"Thanks, Mikoto," Josh said, extending his hand to his ex-roommate and shaking it gratefully.

"No problem." Mikoto moved closer and gave Josh a brief slap on the back. He slammed the back door of his station wagon with a grin, then gave Neptune Avenue's dingy neighborhood a disgusted look. "You and Winnie are out of this lousy place now. Nowhere to go but up."

Josh shrugged and gave his blue earring a nervous spin.

"Yeah," Josh sighed. "Right."

After his blowup with Winnie the day before,

Josh had spent the afternoon and half the night driving around the outskirts of Springfield on his new motorcycle. Somehow, he'd hoped that the wind in his face and the roar of the engine would scour all the anger and frustration out of him.

But when he got back to Lauren's apartment, Winnie wasn't there.

And she'd never come home.

That morning, Josh had jogged miserably over to Forest Hall to see if Mikoto would help him haul their stuff. Although Mrs. Calvin had shoved their belongings unceremoniously into a heap in the lobby, it was still halfway intact. Most of it fit into Mikoto's station wagon. But now he was taking the most useless of Winnie's junk over to the Tri Beta rummage sale he'd seen advertised.

Jamming the last of her stuff into his beat-up backpack, Josh numbly slipped it over his shoulder and hoisted himself onto his bike. His head felt like a tin can, his eyes were bleary, and he had no idea what he was doing. All he knew was that he had to dump off the last of Winnie's stuff and maybe get some rest at their new shoe box of an apartment.

Josh jammed his foot down on the bike's ignition, revved up the engine, and took off down the street.

Over and over, the same questions kept echoing in his foggy head. If he and Winnie loved each other so much, why was everything falling apart so fast? What were they arguing about? Hadn't he been patient enough with her acres of impractical, funky junk? Hadn't he put up with the stupid banners and acted like a saint when she ruined his programming assignment for Dr. Atkins?

The breeze was whistling through Josh's helmet as he leaned into a turn. He had a hot feeling in his eyes that he was trying desperately to shake off. The last thing he needed was to break down in front of a bunch of sorority types.

Where was Winnie last night? She must have slept somewhere. Where?

Josh leaned into a turn and headed down the main drag that bordered the western edge of the campus. He remembered the last time Winnie had checked out on him. It was when her old boyfriend, Travis Bennett, had arrived in town and he'd discovered she'd been seeing both of them at the same time. Just thinking about it made his blood run hot.

Roaring up to the Tri Beta house's side entrance, Josh cut the engine and shoved the kick stand in place.

Had Travis Bennett breezed into town again?

Were her late-night shifts at the hotline really excuses to rendezvous with Travis? Or some other guy?

He was about to take off his backpack and dump Winnie's stuff into a nearby garbage can when he felt something jolt his bike. Jerking his head around, Josh could see that someone had crashed right into the back of his motorcycle and was catching her balance on the driveway.

"Lauren!" Josh called out in surprise when he saw her familiar, round face and wire-rimmed glasses. It looked like Lauren, anyway, although she seemed to be in a daze, lightly brushing off the gravel from her beat-up dungarees.

With shaking hands, Lauren straightened the shoulder strap on her leather purse and slowly turned to look at him. "You're parked in the middle of the driveway, Josh."

The sight of Lauren made Josh's own problems seem smaller. Her eyes were swollen with tears and he could see that she was trying to control the anguish in her face.

"What's happened, Lauren?" he asked, getting off his bike and moving gently toward her. Lauren's dismal apartment would always be a reminder of his rocky start with Winnie, but he knew she'd only tried to help them out after they married so suddenly.

"Nothing. Nothing." Lauren shook her head like a robot with a short circuit, looking down at the laces of her lightweight hiking boots. She sniffed loudly. "What are you doing?"

Josh nodded toward the pack on his back. "Dropping off some of Winnie's stuff at the Tri Beta rummage sale. I—uh—hope she doesn't miss it too much, but Mikoto didn't have any more room in his wagon for the move." Josh gave her a helpless look. "And I—uh—don't know where she is."

Lauren coughed and dug through her purse, finally coming up with a tissue. She blew her red nose loudly. "I was with her last night, Josh. So were Faith and Kimberly. I guess the hotline people were really mad at her when her banners didn't arrive. And she's terrified that you'll get into an accident with that new bike of yours."

Josh looked down and nodded, unable to speak.

"She left town last night . . ."

Josh looked up, scared.

"Who—who did she leave with?" Josh stammered.

"She went with Faith and KC back to Jacksonville in my Jeep," Lauren answered. "KC got a call from home last night. Her dad had a setback. No one would say it, but I think he may be dying."

"Mr. Angeletti?" Josh breathed. He stared absently down the carefully manicured street, with its orderly rows of stately houses. Every star-shaped leaf on every tree was shining and full of life. A soft, warm breeze blew over his face.

"Yeah." Lauren continued to nod, sniffing again. She quickly brushed her cheek with the back of her hand.

"If anything happens to Mr. Angeletti . . ." Josh began softly.

Lauren nodded. "I know. And she's already really upset . . ." Lauren stopped. "Well, you know."

Josh turned, dumped the contents of his back-pack in a collection barrel, and swung a leg up on his motorcycle. Then he fixed his eyes on Lauren's sad face. "You okay?"

"Yeah. Sure I am," Lauren said, turning away with a quick wave. She began walking rapidly toward the dorms. "See you," she called out over her shoulder.

For a few minutes, Josh sat on his bike, dazed. Winnie hadn't run off with another guy. She'd helped take KC to her father's bedside.

"What kind of a jerk am I?" Josh mumbled to himself.

How could he have gone nuts over such ordinary, everyday stuff like packing boxes and oversized banners? He hadn't fallen in love with a moving company or a housekeeper, he'd fallen in love with Winnie. Beautiful, loving Winnie. The girl he could say four words to and she would know exactly what he was saying. The girl who tied her shoes with silver laces and smelled of spring.

He needed Winnie. He wanted to stick by her. The question was, would she ever forgive him?

For richer or poorer, in sickness and in health, till death do us part.

Mr. Angeletti was dying.

The Angelettis and their friends had reason to grieve. He didn't. His life with Winnie was just beginning.

In a few short minutes, Josh's rage had turned into action. Starting up his bike again and rolling it down the Tri Beta side entrance, he quickly checked his wallet. Five bucks. Maybe enough for gas to Jacksonville.

He zipped up his leather jacket and buckled his helmet. He didn't deserve Winnie.

During *his* first week of being married, *he'd* barely thought of anything but his Computer Science 301 homework assignment. *He'd* been the one to walk out in anger twice that week.

And even when he knew Winnie was apartment hunting, *he* hadn't even bothered to tell her what kind of electrical system he needed for his computer. Did he expect her to read his mind?

Slipping on a pair of sunglasses, Josh pushed off from the edge of the sidewalk and headed for the gas station near the freeway entrance.

He'd fill his tank up.

He'd pour caffeinated cola into his tired body.

If he really ripped up the road, he could make it in less than two hours.

When Lauren finally neared the steps to Forest Hall, she was nearly blind with tears and almost tripped over the base of the volleyball net a bunch of barefoot jocks had set up on the warm grass.

"You're blocking the way!" Lauren screamed at the group of startled faces before storming off.

"Take it easy!" she heard one of the tanned guys call out cheerfully as she flung open the door to the lobby.

I detest them. I detest them all! Lauren fumed to herself as she flew up the stairs to her room. She hated everyone. Everything. The rubbery smell of the horrible orange carpeting in the hall. The guy with the know-it-all face walking half-naked out of the men's shower. The perky blond at the hall pay phone. The mindless, cruel, hard rock lyrics that blasted her whenever she passed the third door on the left. She wanted to leave it all and find a place of her own again. Most of all, she wanted to find her life again.

When Lauren reached her room, she stabbed the key in the lock, shoved the door open, and slammed it with all her might.

For once, she was grateful that Melissa always kept the drapes closed. The room was cool, dark, and blessedly quiet. Lauren threw herself down on her bed and let out a deep sound that was somewhere between a sigh and a cry for help. Long, deep sobs began to flood out of her body.

Dash! She loved him, and he was crawling all over Courtney Conner! She'd seen everything: his familiar dark head hovering over Courtney's before it dropped into a kiss. The passionate way he pulled her close. It was horrible! Tri Beta President Courtney Conner! Mistress of sorority row, Courtney Conner! The Courtney Conner who represented everything she and Dash had worked against.

After a few moments, Lauren began to realize that she was not alone in the room. She heard a tiny, faraway sound. The sound of her television set.

Lauren lifted her head up and looked across the room. There in the blue half-light sat Melissa, wearing a beat-up bathrobe and a pair of worn-out gym socks. Her stringy hair had been pulled back into an unattractive ponytail and her sunken eyes were glued to the television screen.

"Hi," Melissa offered in a tired voice. "What happened?"

Lauren flipped herself over angrily. "Oh, nothing. I just dropped by the Tri Beta house to deliver an important message. But it turned out *I* was the one who got the message."

"Huh?" Melissa stirred slightly. "What were you doing over at the Tri Betas? I thought you couldn't stand them."

"*I can't!*" Lauren cried out. "I was just delivering a message for KC when I—when I . . ."

"When you what?" Melissa demanded.

Lauren looked at her in bleary disbelief. For the first time in the week they'd been roommates, Melissa was actually initiating a conversation.

"Hey, forget it," Melissa said, her eyes drifting back to the television. She picked up a half-eaten doughnut off her desk and stuffed the whole thing into her mouth.

"It's Dash!" Lauren blurted. Why not tell Melissa? She'd probably understand better than anyone. "Dash and Courtney. Together."

Melissa looked up. There was a long silence. "I thought you broke up with him."

"Yes, but I wanted to get back together and I thought he did, too!" Lauren wailed.

"Yeah." Melissa shook her head slowly. "Well, what you think they want and what they really want are two completely different things."

"How could I have been so stupid?" Lauren sobbed.

"He's gone. Forever. There's no way I can compete with a girl like Courtney and I'm not going to try."

Melissa narrowed her eyebrows. "You shouldn't have to try."

"What am I going to do?" Lauren cried, feeling her life move away from her as if it were being sucked down a huge black hole.

When she looked across the room, Melissa was staring at her as if she were seeing her roommate for the first time. Slowly, Melissa began to shake her head, but her eyes remained on Lauren. "I wish I could tell you. Nothing's helped me so far."

"Yeah," Lauren sniffed.

"But I'll let you know as soon as I figure it out."

Lauren's tired face bent into a grateful smile.

She watched as Melissa reached behind her and picked up a large white box with one hand.

"Take the last chocolate-glazed in the box," Melissa said, pulling herself up and retying the drooping sash on her old bathrobe. "That's the only suggestion I have so far."

Lauren sighed. "Why not?" She smiled at Melissa. "You bought an entire box of doughnuts—just for yourself?"

"Why not?" Melissa dully echoed her words, moving over on the bed. "Come on. It's *Father Knows Best*."

"Huh?"

"Father Knows Best," Melissa repeated matter-of-factly.

"Good." Lauren settled in. Melissa was turning out to be a perfectly fine roommate after all. Lauren took a large bite out of the fudgy doughnut. "Seen it before?"

"Sure," Melissa said, her eyes welling with tears. "But I've got to do something."

"Yeah, I understand." Lauren chewed, savoring her comforting sugar-chocolate rush.

Melissa reached for another doughnut. "Brooks is coming back to U. of S. tomorrow," Melissa said over the chatter on the television. "He wants to see me."

"Ha!" Lauren blurted, amazed at the confident tone her bitterness was taking on. "The guy has a lot of gall."

Melissa blew her nose loudly, nodding. "Can you believe it? He ruins my life. Then he wants to talk?"

"Forget it," Lauren agreed, pulling another doughnut out of the box.

"Oh, God." Melissa rubbed her nose and shook her head. "At last. Someone who understands."

"I understand," Lauren said.

Melissa stared blankly ahead until the commercial came on. "I hate people who want me to be happy."

"So do I." Lauren kicked off her shoes and stuck a pillow behind her. "Why don't they just leave us in peace?"

Fourteen

"*Dr. Lobrano. 35791. Stat. Dr. Lobrano. 35791. Stat.*"

KC looked wearily into space. Whoever Dr. Lobrano was, he needed to answer his message. Or *her* message. Either that, or maybe Jacksonville Memorial needed to turn off its PA system. There were people here trying to rest.

Just answer the stupid message, she thought irritably, trying to count back the hours since she last slept. Two days? Two weeks? She looked at her digital watch, but it was a blur. She looked down at the family health magazines on the table next to her and suddenly felt sick.

"Here's the candy bar you wanted," Faith said softly as she slumped on a folding chair next to KC in the corridor of the hospital's oncology unit.

"Dr. Lobrano. 35791. Stat. Dr. Lobrano. 35791. Stat."

KC absently peeled away a corner of the foil wrapper. She looked up at Faith's worried face. "Thanks," KC finally said, her voice gravelly from hours of crying.

It was Sunday night. After rushing to Jacksonville the evening before, KC, Winnie, and Faith crashed at KC's house, then left early the next morning for the hospital. Since then, KC had seen her father several times, but each visit had been worse than the last. He'd been unconscious much of the time. And he looked worse than ever.

Bones she never knew he had now outlined his once-robust face. Watching him sleep, it seemed to KC that he was now only a gray, fragile shadow of his former self.

The doctors said he was slipping away peacefully, but it didn't look that way to KC. A needle was stuck in his arm, wires were attached to his chest, and oxygen tubes were snaked into his nose. He looked like a wild bird someone had captured and pinned cruelly to the earth.

"Lydia?" a nurse said in a loud voice, walking

briskly by them. "Check on 315."

There was a long, blissful silence, broken only by the faraway sound of canned television laughter in the waiting room around the corner. Faith and KC were sitting in the hallway to escape it. Winnie was downstairs getting a soda with KC's Grandma Rose.

KC knew her mother wanted her to rest, but there was no way she was going home.

"He'd be angry if he knew what was happening," KC said abruptly. That was the way her mind had been working all day. Thoughts came to her in tiny, painful bursts. Memories. Regrets. Guilt. And when they came, they seemed to spill over, as if she'd lost all ability to hold them in check. It was a strange and dreamlike state, as if her inner thoughts were no longer her own to carefully roll over and shape before she put them into words.

Faith took her hand. "What, KC?"

"He hated doctors and hospitals," KC said softly. "He said they were without soul. That they had no respect for life—or death. He used to get upset about all the money spent keeping people alive on machines when people were going hungry."

Faith squeezed her hand. "I know what you mean."

"Would Mrs. Bastion please return to the surgery waiting area?"

KC stared numbly at an institutional painting hanging on the wall across from her. In the foreground, a white river plummeted down a steep valley that was dotted with stands of Douglas fir and swept with golden grasses. In the background was an enormous snow-covered mountain. Somehow, it reminded KC of all the times her father had awakened her and her brothers at dawn so that he could take them into the mountains surrounding Jacksonville. Picnics. Camping trips. Hikes in autumn to see the brilliantly turning leaves. He wanted them to see it all.

The door to Mr. Angeletti's room opened and KC's oldest brother, Granite, stepped out.

"Hey," Granite said quietly, slipping into a seat next to Faith and KC.

"Hey, Gran," Faith murmured, slipping her arm around his sturdy shoulders.

"What's happening?" KC leaned her elbows on her knees and looked tiredly across at her big brother. Like Mrs. Angeletti, Granite had a thick head of red hair, which he wore in a ponytail down his neck.

"Not good, Kahia." Granite took off his baseball cap and rubbed his forehead. "I can't believe it . . .

but . . . the doctors say he's fading."

Beep. Beep. Beep. Beep. KC heard an alarm in one of the far rooms. Two nurses rushed by. KC covered her face in exasperation.

"The doctors said last week's treatment had absolutely no effect on the tumor," Granite murmured. "Dad can barely breathe now."

KC looked over. "Then why does he seem so peaceful?"

"Morphine." Granite stared down at his worn cowboy boot. "The nurse said it's keeping him from struggling too hard for breath."

KC felt her face begin to shake beneath her hands.

"And I guess the pain's really bad, too," Granite added softly.

KC felt tears dripping between her fingers onto her dress. Faith was gently massaging her back.

"KC? You need to know. He and Mom agreed to a No Code status."

"What?"

"Uh, it means no resuscitation. No crazy blue code teams. It's just comfort care now, KC."

"No. No. *No.*" KC sprang out of her seat. "I have to talk to him."

"You will. You will, KC." Faith took her hand and pulled her back down.

"He wants to tell me something . . ." KC broke off. She paused and tried to breathe and relax.

She waited. A knot was tightening in her stomach from too much coffee and too little sleep. Her head felt disconnected from her body. Down the hall, she could hear the telephone ringing at the nurse's station.

"Oncology. Let me get him for you. Oncology. Please hold. Oncology. I'll send it right down. Please hold. Please hold. Please hold."

After a long while, KC looked over at Granite. "Remember the camping?"

"Yeah." Granite coughed and pulled a red bandanna out of his back pocket, rubbing his whole face with it. "Bighorn Mountain."

A hospital orderly walked by, pushing a rattling, stainless-steel cart. He noisily opened and closed a supply closet across from where they were sitting.

"White River," KC heard herself say. "Camping in the old Volkswagen bus."

Granite sighed. "Never saw a guy who got such a kick out of picking over a field for a few quarts of blueberries."

"Dr. Satran. 50195. Stat. Dr. Satran. 50195. Stat."

"Yeah." KC was staring at a pattern of tiny

indentations in the carpeting. Nothing was making any sense to her. When was her father going to wake up and ask for her? She was waiting for him.

"Why did I complain about his Dead Head tapes and ask him to play classical?" KC said.

Granite looked at her. "He played classical."

"He was just being a sport."

Granite sighed. "He's always respected you, KC. He didn't like it when people tried to fit you into a mold. Even when it was his."

"I couldn't even use the name he gave me." KC shook her head. The inside of her mouth felt like cotton and her whole body was weighted down with sadness and regret.

Just then, the hospital-room door opened and Mrs. Angeletti leaned out. Her eyes were puffy and her lips were dry and colorless. But there was a gentle calm about her. "KC, darling? Would you come back in? Dad's fairly alert now. I think he'd like to see you."

KC stood up as if she were in a dream. The light green walls seemed to be wobbling and a passing group of nurses and doctors appeared to be moving in slow motion. She was exhausted.

She pushed open the door and stepped carefully into the quiet room where her father lay, surrounded by machines, tubes, and monitors.

The shiny linoleum floor clicked beneath her footsteps. Would he tell her about the secret he hinted at the week before? Or would he slowly slip away, leaving her without a good-bye? Leaving her to wonder forever.

KC sat down next to her father while her mother settled at the foot of the bed, a well-worn book of verse on her lap. KC slipped her hand into her father's and studied it carefully, as if for the first time. His was large and square, like her brothers' and her mother's.

Her hands were long and tapered.

Slowly, her father turned his head toward her. His arms were stained purple from the countless IVs. Transparent tubes carrying oxygen to his nose were clamped against his cheeks. But his eyes were still the same. Blue and twinkling.

"Kahia," he whispered, as if he were surprised to see her.

"Yes, Dad." KC's heart was breaking. She had to remind herself to breathe.

"I'm so proud of you," he said faintly.

KC wanted to contradict him. Instead, she gently squeezed his hand.

"This . . ." Mr. Angeletti reached his hand up.

"Mom?" KC looked back in panic.

Her mother stood up and adjusted his oxygen

tube. "It pulls away sometimes," her mother said gently, "and makes him a little uncomfortable."

Mr. Angelleti nodded weakly.

"You don't have to talk, Dad," KC whispered.

"I . . . want to say how proud . . . I am," he began with difficulty. "You're a fighter . . ."

"But, Dad . . ." KC began.

Mr. Angeletti raised one hand up a few inches in protest and shook his head tiredly on the pillow, a slight smile forming on his lips. "You want to . . . argue . . . now . . . with your dad?"

Sick at heart, KC slowly lowered her head down onto the bed, where she let the side of her face rest on the scratchy sheet. No, she didn't want to argue. She just wanted to be close to him. She felt his gentle hand begin to stroke her hair.

"Don't be—afraid," her father began wearily. "I've loved my life . . . "

"No!" KC cried. "Don't talk like that."

"I've . . . got a story," he continued in his barely audible voice. KC's instinct was to make him stop. He looked exhausted. But his eyes were determined, and glued to her face. "It's a story . . . of a happy couple."

Her father closed his eyes and stopped to rest. It seemed as if each breath took a little more life out of him. She could hear it whistling out through his throat.

"They had two boys," he whispered. "So happy . . . a roof over their heads . . . tall trees in back."

KC narrowed her eyes and glanced at her mother, who sat quietly listening. Her dad always liked to tell stories.

"Everything . . . except a girl," he struggled. "A clever girl."

KC's heart was thumping. What was her dad talking about?

"Yet . . . " Mr. Angeletti continued. There was a scary growling in his chest. "So many girls . . . had no home . . ."

KC slowly raised her head and looked into her father's eyes with alarm. She looked over to her mother, who gave her a reassuring nod and touched a finger to her lips.

"So we looked . . . your mother and I." Mr. Angeletti paused a long while to gather his strength. His eyes were closed and his hands were shaking on the bedsheet. KC couldn't breathe. For a moment, she couldn't speak. "Yes. It was us. And—one day, we got a phone call."

"What phone call?" KC said in confusion. "Mom? What's Dad trying to tell me?"

Mr. Angeletti squeezed KC's hand. "A young woman . . . in Portland. She'd just had a beautiful . . . dark-haired baby girl. We drove up . . . and brought her home with us . . ."

KC's face was going numb. She gripped the side of the bed and stared at her father in terror. "The baby . . . was—was me?"

"Yes, sweetheart," she heard her father whisper, as KC felt the room spin and the ground slip out from under her. She felt her mother catch her shoulders and hold her close.

"It's true, Kahia, darling," KC's mother said in a comforting voice. "She was only seventeen. She hadn't even finished high school. She wanted her little girl to have a good home . . . with people who could really care for her."

KC was gasping for breath. The room was suddenly closing in. She thought the smell of disinfectant would suffocate her. "But why?" she sobbed. "Why did you keep it a secret?"

"We didn't plan it that way, darling," her mother said calmly. "We always wanted to tell you when you were young, but we always put it off. It seemed like such a difficult thing for a child to absorb."

"Too much," her father whispered faintly.

"Then," her mother continued, "when you

entered your teens. Well, Kahia. You know that wasn't always easy. We didn't want to make things more difficult for you. So we decided to wait until you were an adult."

"But—but," KC was sobbing in confusion, "how could you keep such a thing a secret? I don't know what to do. I don't know—who I *am*. You led me *on*!"

"But, Kahia . . ." her mother tried to break in, tears forming in her tired eyes.

KC's father was struggling for air. "You are who you are, Kahia."

"But . . . " KC felt her world collapsing in front of her eyes and she couldn't do anything to prevent it.

"Kahia," her father gasped. "If you need to, go ahead and find your natural parents. Please. Do it for me."

"We mean it, Kahia," her mother said gently. "I'll help you, if you want to know someday. There are records . . ."

"No! No!" KC screamed. "*You're* my mother! And *you're* my father."

KC flung herself down next to her father, who had closed his eyes and slipped into unconsciousness. "No one will ever take your place. No one," she sobbed. "*You're* the father I want!"

Fifteen

innie shoved three quarters into the hospital's soda machine and jammed her fist into the cherry-cola button.

With a deep sigh, she took the icy can and walked out into the main lobby of Jacksonville Memorial Hospital, half ignoring the startled stares of the night nurses at the front desk.

She ran a hand through the sticky spikes in her hair and glanced down at her fluorescent orange bodysuit. She probably looked like something out of *Star Trek* to the small-town Jacksonville folks, but she didn't care. She was used to being the hometown oddball.

And right now she felt very much lost in space.

In front of her, the automatic doors flew open for a woman in a wheelchair, carrying a bundled-up newborn in her lap.

Winnie flipped the soda top back and took a long drink. Instinctively, she followed the wheelchair out into the cool spring night. She flopped down on the front steps of the old hospital and watched the woman's cheerful husband roll her down the ramp, happily joking and talking and gazing down at the tiny bundle.

There were still people out there actually experiencing joy, Winnie thought wistfully, wondering if she'd ever feel anything again.

It was nearly midnight. Winnie had been with KC, Faith, and KC's family at the hospital since early morning. For hours, Winnie had been sitting in the corridor of Jacksonville Memorial's antiseptic oncology unit, feeling her legs go gradually numb and her mind turn to fog. The whole terrible situation had left her feeling helpless and terrified.

But she still hoped she'd helped KC a little. If nothing else, she'd been there to deliver stale cups of instant coffee and tell the morons in the waiting room to turn down the television.

She thought about KC's ragged face, her wild, unkempt hair and bloodshot eyes. KC hadn't taken the day well at all. Mrs. Angeletti and the two Angeletti brothers had been serene. But KC had seemed to need something more.

Why did hospitals have to be so mean-looking? The walls were gray. The carpets were gray. Even the chrome on the gurneys and the chairs looked cruel and inhuman. Wasn't there a way they could cover up the machines and instruments and strange, awful smells?

Winnie hugged herself against the cool night air and began to cry. Not since her high school friend had been in the motorcycle accident had she come into such close contact with suffering and death. And this time it was even more real—and final.

Now, all she longed for was Josh. She felt lost and weary, like a wandering molecule in deep space with no attachments. No purpose. No love. Would they ever find a way to come together?

She thought briefly of picking up the phone and calling her mom. But she didn't want to analyze things with her analyst mother.

She wanted to talk to Josh.

"What am I doing?" Winnie whispered to herself, cradling her head in her arms, unable to stop crying.

In the last few hours, Winnie had begun to understand a lot of things. About family. About loyalty. About people facing life together, bravely. All day, the Angelettis had been proving to her how important those things were. She longed for the same kind of closeness and affection. The whole day reminded her painfully of what she'd never really had.

Winnie stared down at the shiny bells dangling from her leather boots and took another gulp of her cherry cola. Cars occasionally pulled past her. Over and over, the ding of the automatic hospital doors rang out into the night.

The day had been terrible, but at least it had left her with a fuzzy vision of the life she wanted to live. She just had to quit getting sidetracked on the unimportant stuff. She knew now that her happiness was all tied up with Josh's. But would they waste their lives struggling over who was right and who was wrong?

Winnie stood up and walked toward a garden bench she'd spotted on the hospital grounds near the emergency entrance. Above, the sky was thick with millions of stars.

Would Josh ever give her another chance? Was he as confused as she was? How much could they expect from each other? How much should they have to give up?

Winnie's heart stopped cold when she spotted something shiny and familiar near the emergency entrance. There, in the dim light, she could see what looked like Peter Dvorsky's motorcycle lying on its side, strewn haphazardly across two parking spaces.

"Josh!" Winnie cried out, jumping up from the bench and racing toward the emergency door. "Josh!"

Racing across the lawn, Winnie's knees were shaking and she was nearly blinded by tears of panic and confusion. Her only thought was that Josh had somehow followed her to Jacksonville and had crashed in the parking lot when he reached the hospital. How long had he been there? Had he hurt himself badly? Did the medics have to carry him inside?

"Josh!" Winnie screamed.

"Winnie!" she heard a voice yell back in the semidarkness. "Winnie! Where are you?"

"Josh!" Winnie sobbed, reaching for him as he approached. "What are you doing here? Are you okay?"

Slowly, tenderly, Josh wrapped his arms around her. Winnie pressed her cheek against the soft cotton of his sweatshirt.

"I'm okay," Josh said gently, holding her close. "Lauren told me that you drove over here with Faith and KC. And—and I just wanted to make sure you were okay."

"Your bike . . ." Winnie began as Josh threw his leather jacket around her shoulders and led her toward the hospital entrance.

Josh looked back at the overturned motorcycle. "Yeah. I guess I was in kind of a hurry to find you, but I went in the wrong entrance. How's—how's Mr. Angeletti?"

Winnie felt her eyes sting and her face crumple once again. She stopped and hugged Josh around the waist. "He died an hour ago, Josh."

Josh's mouth parted, then closed again when his eyes met Winnie's. "I'm sorry, Win. I'm sorry about everything."

"He's gone and I'll never get to talk to him again," Winnie said bitterly. Tears were flooding out of her eyes and she couldn't stop shaking.

"I know. It hurts," Josh soothed, stroking the spiky nest of her hair. "What do you say we get out of here? You need some rest."

"What are we going to do, Josh?" Winnie said, continuing to shake from nerves and fatigue. "I mean, I'm sorry about everything, too, but I'm just having trouble figuring everything out. Maybe I—I don't know how to be married, Josh. Maybe I never will."

"It's not easy. I've got a lot to learn, too." Josh was sliding his hand back and forth across her neck, looking up at the sky.

Winnie rubbed her eyes tiredly. "I don't have any experience, Josh. I never lived with a mom and dad who had to work things out. It was just me and my mom doing our own thing. Now that I look back on it, it was no problem, compared to being married."

"Yeah, I know."

"It's just that I love you so much, Josh," Winnie said in a rush. "And—and I guess I know that we don't have forever. Everything comes to an end."

"Yeah."

"No," Winnie said, taking deep breaths as she cried into Josh's shoulder. The wet grass was making her feet cold, but she didn't care. "Do you understand? I mean, everyone *says* they understand that we all die. And that we only have so much time. But it's really true, Josh. It just doesn't hit you until you've seen it right before your eyes."

Josh stroked Winnie's face. "We'll work things out, Winnie. I know we can," he said. "We decided that last weekend."

Winnie felt Josh take her left hand in his and hold it up to his mouth. Softly, he brushed her gold wedding band with his lips. "Remember this?"

Winnie slipped her arms around Josh's waist and glued her body tight to his. She could have stood there in the middle of the wet grass all night long.

"It won't be easy, Win," Josh whispered. "But we'll work it out together. I want to."

"I do, too," Winnie whispered. "Let's start all over. Starting right now."

Here's a sneak preview of the big, fabulous Freshman Dorm Super, FRESHMAN SUMMER.

*T*he ocean was a clear turquoise.

The sand was white and glistened in the sun.

Faith paused on the shore of Dolphin Cove to breathe in the sweet sea air. She found it hard to believe that there were any environmental problems on the island. But, she knew better. Marissa O'Neil's talk that morning had struck home.

Hawaii was a fragile paradise, and the very beauty that attracted tourists might lead to the overdevelopment that was already causing terrible destruction. Faith's resolve to protect this beautiful place from further environmental damage deepened. Like the other strong swimmers in the group, Faith's task for the morning involved spotting dolphins that inhabited the cove, counting those which were already tagged, and noting how many were not.

"Dolphins!" KC's excited voice carried on the breeze. "Look!"

Faith shaded her eyes and peered out to sea just as a small school of dolphins broke the surface. The five silver bodies leapt in perfect unison high into the blue sky and hung suspended a moment, like dancers doing grand jetés, before they plummeted joyfully back into the water. Then several of the dolphins surfaced again, barely skimming the waves. They seemed to look right at the straggly row of students wading out from the shore. Faith got the crazy feeling they wanted all onlookers to jump in and join in their games.

Now she understood why Marissa had said that dolphins regarded humans as playmates and equals. Faith couldn't wait a moment longer to see one up close and perhaps even be brave enough to touch it. She pulled her goggles down over her eyes and plunged into the ocean.

The salt water was buoyant and her powerful strokes soon brought Faith out a good distance.

She treaded water and readjusted her goggles. Suddenly, there was a glint in the sun, a flash of blue. Faith's heart pounded in anticipation. "I found one!" she yelled. But she was too far away for anyone else to hear. She gulped down a lung full of air and with a strong kick of her legs, dove beneath the slightly choppy surface.

A blue-green world of waving kelp and sculptured coral greeted her. The water was so clear she could see for yards. Indifferent to her presence, a school of striped angel fish swam right in front of her and through a fantastic coral arch. It wasn't until her lungs burned for air that Faith remembered to surface. She stayed up only long enough to gulp down more oxygen, and this time aimed herself more carefully in the general direction of the dolphin she had spotted.

Suddenly she saw it again—a sliver of blue cutting through the water just ahead. She swam underwater in its wake. A few more strokes and she could touch it. Then its fin turned into an arm and a powerful hand reached back and gripped her wrist.

One swift yank upwards and Faith surfaced.

"HEEELLLP!" she screamed into the wind. Every horror movie she had ever seen seemed to be coming true.

"It's okay!" the person who had grabbed Faith shouted. "I thought you were in trouble." It was a man's voice. He shoved his goggles on top of his head, and a pair of sea-green eyes met Faith's. They were full of concern and fringed with dark lashes. His pale blond hair dripped in a ponytail down his back.

Faith only nodded as her heart began to slow down. She felt ridiculously stupid, mistaking a neoprene-clad swimmer for a dolphin. And she felt annoyed at him, for just being there, and for *not* being a dolphin.

Faith freed herself from his grasp and flashed him a quick noncommittal smile. Then she began to swim further out to sea. He followed her.

Faith dove to escape him. He dove after her.

Faith turned on him, waving him away. He paused and arched gracefully under the water and changed direction, heading more toward shore. A few strokes later, he turned to see if she was following.

Faith's heart began to beat faster. Crazy fairy tales she and Winnie used to make up about Mermen flashed through her mind. He seemed magical and from another world. Suddenly, she sped after him, and managed to touch his foot just as he surfaced. She continued swimming underwater an instant longer, then came up for air. He was waiting, just as she sensed he would be. A strand of kelp had twisted in his hair and his tanned shoulders shone in the sun.

They locked glances only an instant this time before he coursed off at top speed. Faith tore after him, but just as she neared him he whirled gracefully in the water, and once again grabbed her hand. He didn't pull her closer, but began to dive down. Faith followed in what felt like a wonderful dance. They surfaced, still holding hands. Their faces were just inches from each other. He pushed up his goggles, then hers, and tilted her face toward his. Faith's heart stopped.

A shrill whistle pierced the air. The moment was shattered.

Faith dropped the stranger's hand.

Marissa in her red tank suit waved broadly from shore and blew her whistle three more times. Faith cut through the waves back into the calmer water of the cove and came up on the far end of the beach. Keeping her back to the ocean, she ran her hands down her face, wiping off the water. Then she bent over to wring out her sopping hair. When she straightened up, the stranger was standing in front of her, a frayed

Superman beach towel in his hand. He offered her a corner.

Faith hesitated a moment. She was confused, a little frightened and very embarrassed. She, Faith Crowley, had just shared a very intimate moment with a hunk of a guy she hadn't even really met yet.

"Thanks," she said, wiping her face dry and looking at him again. His wet suit was half unzipped, revealing a muscular body.

He smiled. "Sorry I scared you out there."

"Sorry I reacted like a madwoman. I thought you were . . ." Faith paused as she noticed the small tattoo on his left upper arm. It was of a dolphin arching through a rainbow. And it was an omen—a lucky omen. Faith was sure of it. "It's silly, but I thought you were a dolphin turned sea monster for a minute."

They both laughed.

"You're a wonderful swimmer," he told her easily.

"Thanks, you look like you were born in the water," Faith said. He really did look like a sea god, with kelp still tangled in his hair and droplets of water shining on his golden tan.

"I've lived here my whole life," he said. "You

sort of get thrown into the ocean before you can walk, living on an island like this."

"You grew up here?" Faith asked, her blue eyes round with surprise. "In the middle of all this?" She threw her arms open to the sky, the trees, the softly scudding waves.

He gave a so-what sort of shrug.

"You're lucky. I'd give anything, absolutely anything to have grown up here. It's such a magical place."

"Magical to you. *Boring* to me," he said, brushing the sand off his legs.

Faith blinked. "You've got to be kidding!"

"No. Where are you from? I bet it beats this place any day."

Faith had to laugh. "I don't think you'd say that if you ever visited my hometown. I grew up in Jacksonville, Oregon. Now I live on campus at the University of Springfield in Oregon."

His eyes sparkled with interest. "Hey, isn't that up in the mountains?"

Faith nodded.

"That's the life," he said. "I'd love to visit a place like that. I haven't been—"

"FAITH!" KC shouted, jogging up. Her hair hung in damp perfect strands, and even wet and sandy she looked beautiful. She planted herself right next to Faith and frowned at the sight of the guy. "Come on," she urged. "Marissa wants you back with the group."

"But . . ." Faith didn't quite know what to do. She wanted to introduce KC to her new friend but she didn't know his name. And before she could ask him, KC dragged her a few feet down the beach.

"Really Faith, where did you dredge up that guy? He's no dolphin and he's certainly no Fire Prince. More like a beach bum if I've ever seen one," KC said in an undertone. "He's probably crashing this scene. We should warn Marissa. I can't believe you'd even *talk* to some guy with a tattoo."

"KC, would you shut up!" Faith ordered in a whisper. She sensed that the stranger from the water was right behind them. Had he overheard every word of KC's put-down? Faith turned around to see, and at that moment he passed them without a glance.

"So crew, how did your first day go?" Philip Cannon greeted everyone as they straggled to the gathering point higher up on the beach.

"Great!"

"We saw five tagged dolphins and two not!"

"The scuba team is still tagging," Marissa updated everyone. "I told them to come back in another half-hour or so."

"Good," Philip said. "We'll all meet back at the hotel for lunch, and by then the scuba team will have its report. I think this is going to be the start of a very promising working vacation for all you students, and for us here at It's Our Earth headquarters."

KC touched Faith's hand. Faith looked at KC and saw that her friend's cheeks were pink from excitement and her eyes were wide as she looked straight ahead at Philip.

Philip jumped down off the bench, then snapped his fingers. "Wait, please. I forgot something very important. Actually, we at Cannon Resorts invited a very special guest to help with this round of workshops, and I'd like to introduce him. He's one of our favorite local celebrities, Hawaii's top amateur surfer, Davis Mattingly." He gestured into the crowd.

"Oh no!" KC moaned. "I blew it!"

Faith caught her breath. Her sea god jumped up on the bench next to Philip and waved obligingly to the group.

Everyone applauded.

"Yo Davis!" someone yelled.

"Right on. Are you in the competition coming up?"

Davis Mattingly nodded and grinned but didn't say anything.

"Davis Mattingly," Faith murmured softly. She liked the sound of his name. "Davis," she said again, a little louder. Then she looked up and waved, and smiled and tried to catch his eye.

For a moment their glances met, then purposefully and coldly Davis turned his back on Faith and followed Philip Cannon to the jeep that awaited him. The language of his perfect surfer's body told Faith all she needed to know. He had heard KC call him a beach bum. He had overheard everything.

"Faith, I didn't mean it, really I didn't," KC told her as they slowly moved down the buffet line back at the resort. Two long tables spread with fruit and salads and cold cuts and cheese lined either side of the hotel's open air dining area.

"Whether you meant it or not," Faith said tightly, "he heard you. I meet this guy, a really cute guy—maybe not your idea of a fire prince, but maybe, just maybe mine—" Faith broke off. "Oh, never mind, KC. Sometimes apologies aren't enough. I know you're sorry, but that won't change a thing. He sure won't look at me again." She led the way toward one of the back tables that didn't face the beach.

"I wouldn't say that," KC said. She followed Faith, though she kept looking back over her shoulder to where Davis Mattingly and Philip Cannon were eating at one of the front tables. This was her chance to re-connect with the young, handsome, and wealthy resort owner. She didn't want some stupid argument with Faith to get in the way. "After all," she said as they put their trays on the broad, wood planked table. "You just have to take matters into your own hands if you want something to happen. I'm sure you can patch it up with him if you try."

"Ms. Patch-It to the rescue again," quipped Winnie as she came up to the table and sat down with them. "Where were you when Lauren's car broke down last week and her spare went flat?"

KC shook her head at Winnie, who began to giggle. "Really, KC," Winnie said. "If we all didn't love you, we'd probably hate you by now."

"Tell me about it," Faith grumbled into her Paradise Papaya salad.

"That's not fair," countered KC. "The two of you are ganging up on me."

"Yeah, but you deserve it," Winnie said solemnly. "Somehow you think everything can be made better." Then she cracked a smile. "And you're right, of course. KC *Angel*etti has wings and always lands on her feet."

KC shook her head. "Not true. I don't always land on my feet, not without the help of my friends."

"I was getting to that," Winnie said. She smiled at Faith and they both giggled.

"Okay, okay. Make fun of me. But I mean what I say. You've got to take the initiative, Faith. Don't give up so easily. If you want Davis Mattingly, go after him. I for one have no intention of waiting around when it comes to a certain Mr. P.C." She dabbed her mouth with her napkin, pulled out a mirror, fixed her lipstick, then stood up and ran her fingers through her dark wavy hair. Turning one more time to her friends, she flashed a victory smile, then with all the dignity and confidence she could muster, walked off to charm Philip Cannon.

He had finished eating and was standing by

the lobby's reception desk, talking to a clerk. KC waited quietly until the girl turned to put away some keys.

"Mr. Cannon—" KC began.

He turned around. The look of vague annoyance on his face gave way to something else. KC thought he almost looked pleased. "Oh, hello. It's you."

His response startled her. "You remember me!" KC gasped, then inwardly kicked herself. "We—we haven't really been introduced," she said, conjuring up a more formal tone. "I'm KC—"

"Angeletti," he interrupted, leaning back with his elbow against the desk. "I remember your nametag. How do you like your It's Our Earth experience so far, KC?"

"It's great," KC said enthusiastically. "I really enjoyed being in the water this morning and getting some hands-on experience as an animal-behavior field worker." KC stopped and forced herself to gather her thoughts. She couldn't afford to waste this opportunity talking about stuff that wasn't important to her plan. Though with those piercing eyes staring right at her, it took a moment to remember exactly why she had approached Philip in the first place.

He shifted to the other foot, obviously waiting for her to say something. "Actually, I wanted to ask you a favor," KC said.

One eyebrow shot up. Philip didn't say anything, but his smile encouraged her to continue.

KC took a deep breath. "As you know, our university is supposed to give us course credit for our work here. I'd love to do something extra and interview you about your work with Cannon Resort. I'd like to know more about Cannon's leadership in the recycling program, and how your participation in the It's Our Earth program works in terms of good business."

Philip's shoulders tightened slightly, and KC wondered what she had said wrong. She quickly hurried on. "Of course I know you don't have much time, but I'm really interested in making environmental work profitable. I'm a business major."

Philip seemed to relax. "I like that idea. About making environmental efforts profitable. I'm just a little surprised someone your age has thought so much about it." He cocked his head and seemed to study her for a moment. "But I shouldn't be surprised." He stood up straight and stepped a little closer to KC. "In fact, KC, I think talking with you could be very interesting.

Not everyone on this island understands my motives in It's Our Earth."

"I think I will," KC said from the bottom of her heart.

"How about talking over lunch? It'll have to be late, around three, and not tomorrow, but the next day," he said, consulting the small date book he had pulled from his pocket.

KC smiled. "I'm free whenever you have the time."

"Good." Philip put out his hand. KC took it and gave it a firm handshake. "I'll look forward to this," he said.

KC smiled again and walked out of the lobby. She forced her feet to stay glued to the gravel as she proceeded down the hibiscus lined path that led to the sundeck and the whale-shaped pool.

Lauren was there, and Faith, and Winnie. Josh was dripping by the side of the pool, toweling his hair off. KC kept her cool until she was absolutely sure Philip Cannon couldn't see her. Then she leapt into the air and let out a loud, happy yell.

"I DID IT. I DID IT."

Faith hugged her first. "You're amazing, KC. One look from you and Philip Cannon is probably talking drivel."

KC looked smug. "I was talking to him now. But I'm going to have *lunch* with him in two days." She sank back against the table and let her knees sag. "Can you believe it?"

"KC the Magnificent pulls it off," Winnie declared. "Where? When? How? What will you wear?"

"Hold it, Winnie. Give KC a chance to answer," cried Lauren, joining the other girls in a great group hug. "Tell us exactly how you did it. I think we all need a lesson."

"Did what?" Josh asked, walking up. He had a baffled expression on his face. "KC, what happened to you? You look radiant!"

KC stared at him and giggled. "Oh, you men!" she said. Then she threw her arms around Josh and planted a big lipsticky kiss on his cheek. "Now I know why you married him!" she told Winnie. "No one ever called me radiant before!"

"Well, my *husband* has never used that word to describe me," Winnie said. "I guess I'm not the radiant type."

"Come on, Win. Don't tell me you're jealous?" Josh teased, hitting her playfully with the wet towel.

"Hmmm," Winnie replied, rolling her eyes. "*Moi*, jealous? Never."

"Good," Faith said, picking up her video camera from a lounge chair. "Because I want KC and Josh to kiss again." She flicked on the power switch. "Rolling," she warned. "Now play it one more time. Steam it up!"

This time when KC grabbed Josh, she kissed him right on the lips.

And Winnie wasn't smiling.

*Don't miss this exciting mystery
from HarperPaperbacks
A Mollie Fox Mystery
Double Dose
created by Peter Nelson*

"*I*'d like to live up here, wouldn't you?" Roberta Baldwin pointed at a huge mansion. It looked more like a castle than someone's home. "I bet even the servants have servants."

Seventeen-year-old Mollie Fox smiled and shifted gears in her Jeep as they climbed the hill toward the area known in Bayside as "The Heights." Only the very wealthy could afford to live there, with the view of San Francisco Bay right out their kitchen windows. "Yeah, it's nice, but imagine the clothes you'd have to wear. Corduroy pants, sweaters with those queer little flowery patterns around the neck—"

"Not me," Roberta said. "If I was rich, I'd still be the fashion plate I am now—only I'd give my clothes away to poor folk like you after I'd worn them once."

Mollie laughed and looked at her friend. Roberta was thin, beautiful, and definitely had her own style. She often wore big sweaters over her multicolored leggings and cowboy boots. Today her dark skin and brown eyes stood out against an oversized red silk blouse.

"Do you think Meredith will be home?" Roberta asked.

"Where else would she be?" They pulled into Meredith Hughes's driveway, and Mollie stopped the car.

"I don't know. Shopping? Cruising around in her Miata?"

"I doubt it," Mollie said. "She's probably trying to keep a low profile. Anyway, she can't go too far—she's out on bail, remember?"

Meredith had been busted for carrying cocaine in her suitcase on a recent trip back from New York City. Mollie knew Meredith wasn't a drug user, so the only explanation was that her friend had been set up. One question kept bugging her, though: Why would anyone bother framing a high-school student?

"Yeah, I know she's out on bail," Roberta said. "Hey, check it out—her father's trying to get into politics."

Mollie looked at the front lawn, which sprawled down to Highland Drive. On it was a big blue sign that said DRAFT HUGHES. "That's not her father, that's her uncle," Mollie said. "Dayton Hughes." She parked the Jeep in front of the house and hopped out. "People want him to run for governor. Pretty amazing, considering he's never done anything for the public good before."

"Not really—I mean, look at California's most famous governor." Roberta got down from the Jeep, and she and Mollie went up to the front door. "The only experience Reagan had was acting in a bunch of B-movies. And he made it all the way to the White House."

"Good point," Mollie said. Just as she was about to rap the large brass lion's-head knocker against the door, it opened. Derek Hughes, Meredith's father, stepped outside.

"Hello, girls," he greeted them. "What are you doing here?" As usual, he was dressed in a navy-blue suit with a red tie—typical boring lawyer fashion. And, of course, he was carrying a monogrammed leather briefcase.

"Hi, Mr. Hughes. We came to see Meredith," Roberta said.

"We thought she could use a friend or two," Mollie added.

"Actually, I think it's best if she doesn't see anybody right now," Mr. Hughes said. "She's quite upset."

"Maybe if we talk to her—"

"I don't think so." Derek Hughes shook his head. "Not today, anyway. Now, if you don't mind, I need to get to the office. Why don't you call Meredith tomorrow, after she's had time to rest."

Rest from what? Mollie wondered. But since Derek Hughes was blocking the door, there was only one thing to do. "Okay, Mr. Hughes. Thanks. Tell her we hope she's feeling better about things," Mollie said.

Roberta gave Mollie an are-you-crazy look, but she followed Mollie to the Jeep. They got in and backed out of the driveway. "I don't feel right, not seeing Meredith," Roberta finally said.

"Don't worry," Mollie assured her as she flipped the radio dial.

"What do you mean, don't worry? Meredith was *arrested* yesterday. She might have to do time in one of those juvenile places where the girls have huge muscles and box for entertainment. You *know* she wouldn't last long there."

Mollie laughed. "Chill already, we're not abandoning her." She turned left onto Highland Drive. Then she made a U-turn and parked the Jeep alongside the right side of the road, under some trees that shaded the car from view.

"I get it," Roberta said. "When Hughes leaves, we go back."

Mollie nodded. "There's no way we're not going to see her today. I mean, if we found a way to get out of a collapsed mall after an earthquake, we can figure out how to get in to see Meredith."

Mollie had moved to Bayside only about a year ago, but already she had a close group of friends—unofficially dubbed the "Mall Rats"—because they'd been trapped underground when a big earthquake hit. They'd dug out just in time to hear their eulogies. Then they'd sworn revenge on the sleazy boss who had left them to die. In the aftermath, a tight bond between the seven teenagers had been formed. Mollie would do anything for any of them, and she knew it went both ways.

A few minutes later, a midnight-blue Mercedes sedan pulled out of the driveway, turned right, and headed off down the road. "Check it out, his car matches his suit," Roberta commented as Mollie backed out toward the Hugheses' mansion. "Hey, what about her mother? She might be home."

Mollie shook her head. "Mrs. Hughes is in Hawaii

for a month. Meredith told me her parents can't stand each other." They parked, and Mollie killed the engine and pocketed the keys. "Just to be safe, let's go around to the back. Meredith spends a lot of time by the pool."

"Can you imagine having your own pool?" Roberta asked.

"No," Mollie said frankly. "My little sister Rosemary has a pretty cool wading pool, though. It's pink plastic."

"Nice," Roberta said. "You'll have to invite me over for a dip."

In back of the house was a kidney-shaped pool with turquoise and pink tiles, surrounded by a high wooden fence. Mollie unlatched the gate, and they walked in. "See, I told you she would be out here." She pointed to a girl with long chestnut brown hair, sitting in a lounge chair, with one leg dangling in the water.

"Meredith!" Roberta called.

The girl looked over at them and slid her sunglasses down her nose. She didn't acknowledge them with a wave.

Mollie and Roberta walked closer. "That's not a girl, that's a woman," Mollie whispered. "She's at least thirty-five."

"You're not Meredith," Roberta said to the woman.

"Thank God. My name's Rahel. Can I help you girls with something?"

"We're here to see Meredith. We go to school with her, and we, uh, brought an assignment for her. It's really important, so the teacher wanted to make sure she got it today," Mollie said.

"She's inside," Rahel replied.

"Are you her cousin or something?" Roberta asked.

Rahel rolled her eyes. "No. I'm one of her father's

clients. I'm a model. Derek handles my money."

I wonder if that's all he handles, Mollie thought, looking Rahel over. She was absolutely gorgeous, and since Mr. and Mrs. Hughes were practically separated, anything was possible. "So you're just here hanging out?" Mollie asked.

"Actually, I'm living down at the guest house for a while," Rahel said.

Mollie nodded. "Well, I guess we'll go find Meredith."

"Go ahead, but she's not in a very good mood," Rahel warned. She slipped her sunglasses back on and tipped her face up to the sky.

"Doesn't she know the sun will shrivel her up and kill her modeling career?" Roberta commented as they stepped through a sliding glass door into the Hugheses' spacious living room.

"Probably not. Anyway, I hear the alligator-skin look is really hot in Paris this year."

"Who's there?" a voice called out.

"Us, Mollie and Roberta."

Meredith walked out of the kitchen, carrying a can of diet soda in one hand and a bag of chips in the other. "Hi. Did you guys come in the back?"

Mollie nodded.

"Why?"

"Never mind," Mollie said. "We just wanted to see how you're doing."

Meredith sank into a big black leather chair by the fireplace. "I'm fine." She took a chip out of the bag and crunched it in her mouth.

"What happened?" Mollie asked.

Meredith stared at the floor and shoved another chip into her mouth.

"If you're fine, then I'm white," Roberta said, sitting down next to Meredith. "Say, I've never seen you eat junk food like this in your entire life. You've got to be in trouble."

Meredith sighed. "I am."

"So what *happened*?" Mollie asked again. "We know you're not a cokehead, so somebody must have been trying to get you busted."

"Yeah, and it obviously worked," Roberta added. "Now if you don't tell us what happened, we can't help you prove you didn't have anything to do with that nose candy in your bag."

Meredith was chewing her thumbnail. "Okay, I'll tell. But I don't want you guys to think you have to save me. I mean, my dad's a really good lawyer and I'm sure he'll get the charges dropped."

Mollie wasn't so sure. Her father was a detective on the Bayside police force, and she knew they were trying to crack down on drug users and dealers. They didn't just let people go, not without incredibly airtight proof.

🏛 HarperPaperbacks *By Mail*